EMPYREAN EMPIRE

VESA M. LUMIELLE

www.resverie.com

Softcover ISBN: 978-9925-7657-0-6
E-book ISBN: 978-9925-7657-1-3

Interior design by Deborah Perdue, Illumination Graphics

CHAPTER 1

Breathe and close those eyes, she hears.

In a dream, she is closing her eyes and entering a time 35,000 years ago. A valley arises in the mists of the majestic mountain range, covered with the prism of secrets. Alive then, forgotten in the essence of continuance.

From the fog, a sharp, authoritative triangle emerges. The focus centers on the Black Pyramid: an interstellar ship that is also a temple, capable of travel across far distances and all dimensions; its presence is overwhelming, as if it demands an audience for the mystery it holds. Traveling deeper into the depths of the dark temple, an alchemist is setting up an experiment: the Alchemist adapting energies in a micro-creature. A dedicated final project. "Will it be my name written in the hearts of Atlanteans?" His outspoken character evident as he relishes mental images of the kneeling, submissive priest-and-priestess class.

The emptiness, the loneliness, is reflected in his eyes, signaling a dark prospect for the future—the hallucination of the madness he's entered.

Upon completion, the plan will be successful, the excitement amplified by the blood's circulation of the nanocrystals. They aren't a few but an army of powerful dark beings. The pyramid is inhabited by a variety of entities: snakelike, reptilian, humans, and creatures of mixed genetics. Some created for a purpose, some for experiment and amusement.

His ambition is to redesign, redirect, the fate of the human race, open it to an agenda for the coming time. The strategy involves cycles of motion; soon the critical movements are revealed. The Alchemist is standing tall in the laboratory provided him. His matted black cloak compliments the desire to deliver his vengeance from the aspect ruling him currently: anger and hatred when contemplating the possible outcome and emotional reward.

The silver pendulum swinging, patterning images in the astral field, his fractured skin and the violet fingers reveal a history of painful poison that once circulated in his body. He holds the silver chain while disturbed symbols in the pendulum pull it, scattering black dust-like material in the space between dimensions. The substance of ancient magicians, promotion of an existing essence or a spark of demise, paste of reality: "the hollow sand." He looks out at the valley of Atlantis. A full moon enhances her presence, lighting the glossy black surface of the pyramid. "Time to capture the crystal moon." His intention rushed from head to toe like lighting striking, an eye toward the moon while reflecting the thought before moving to his desk.

Focusing the pendulum laser into the alchemy of metallurgy. Particles in this dust cloud are rare metals and crystals binding together, creating a cocktail of nano-sized intruders— the laser seeding knowledge to each of the particles produced. Each organism knows its function, processing its capacity to be modified and evolve. The Alchemist breathes slowly, examining the tank. The seed of destruction is prepared. "Instrumental to establishing the new order in Atlantis," he adds. When the black robe with the full hood is covering him, one can feel the luster of his wicked success. Black blood is circulating in his body. Injured severely in an explosion in the past, his blood vessels expand under the influence of the chemical injected to keep his molecular structure together. The laboratory is made from a black crystal substance; not a crystal from the stars, but one created from the hollow sand; it has an extraordinary capability to migrate between dimensions and serve as a charge in the resonance field of the *Black Pyramid*—a protective layer for the Order of Black Pyramid, allowing it to stay hidden between dimensions when needed. He is on a particular mission— injustice to be balanced, a ruling society of the priest class established. "Eons ago they destroyed my desire," he remembers. It's something he can share inside the Order.

Evolving the human race would leave a great legacy under his name, and perhaps his daughter, seeing what a great man he is, would return to him. He is sure that this significant an achievement would restore his reputation and give him the position he had been craving for lifetimes." In the next life, things will be dictated by me, not anyone else," he added while watching his image in the crystal mirror—perceiving in the shadows of the glass reflection an alien creature staring at him, a being with whom he joined to fulfill his ambition. This creature has full control of him when wanted, sometimes delivering a message with enormous physical and mental pain. The Alchemist stands frozen cold as his "good deed" voice takes over the mind complex and bombards him with soft, childlike, compelling messages to use his skills for a higher reality. His rage boils up, and the voice is gone. "I am going to take care of this very soon," he promises and shakes the moment off.

Qali steps into the gleaming, "out of this world" corridor in this pyramid labyrinth, his steps echoing in the hallway as he makes his way toward the Black Queen. It takes intuition to learn to maneuver intersections in transforming space.

The design was specially constructed to confuse intruders in case unwanted energies find their way here. Each step leads to another corridor, each passage multiplied in an identical passage. A random shuffle occurs, and the labyrinth reorganizes however the computer decides.

The crystal implants are connected to the ship's computer, updated with the newest blueprint. Qali is moving toward the chamber, and the hollow sand stimulants the Alchemist objected to vibrate stronger, blending the physical and etheric dimensions. Without proper training, he cannot move closer or he'd be in jeopardy of crossing timelines. "This point forward is a testimony to my greatness, beyond the natural limit of skilled individuals. Qali bathed in his self-confidence, while mildly moving his hand in front of the door. "Access Granted!" he felt. Colossal doors open into the area, patterned by abstract yet geometric forms. A community of confusion; lighting provides little help to understand the concept. In the middle of the room stands his Queen, the Black Queen, insurgent in her own way. The choice she made after the collapse of second Atlantis.

"Queen, I'm here, ready to forward the experimental substance," Qali informed submissively. Silence, the unique ambiance, covering the space as her eyes capture the soul and essence of Qali. "You are not here for that, my Alchemist; we are relocating, and I wanted to travel with you," she informed him with a captivating, soft voice.

Before Qali could reply in any possible way, the *Pyramid* started to vibrate, reverberate, and shake. The feeling mutually occupying Qali. The reality melted away as the walls dissolved in the dimension behind him; an unknown energy of matter became absolute, as well the essence of his Queen! Qali's existence was thrust violently forward by the spinning consciousness, and thousands of lightning strikes were hitting him and escorting him to the reality of no matter and consciousness.

CHAPTER 2

Incandescent view, the bewilderment of Lake Sirius; the mirror-like reflection of the Golden Sun materializes as dancing stillness in the little vortex of solar life. A stream of sunrays gently carries the thought in the tranquility of expansion. His breath, in a union with the soul, gently drawing the invisible painting of love into his heart. Admiring the moment sliding in the present. Air transits oxygen and richness of love, dressing the body with the nutrients of joy.

The Earth under his bare skin is a magnetizing body as vibrations gently arise from the ground. The flow of the union of spirits is centered in its core in the harmony of regeneration. The dimension of time fades elsewhere from a Oneness perspective, as the vibration climbs to the climax and the bluster of today settles down. Radiance fulfills presence.

In his eyes opens the majestic view of alluring nature, a vast calm lake, the imperial mountains in a concert with the wind, this portrait complimented by the setting Sun and two moons: Crystal and Stardust. Under the hills is a classic mix of colors, ruled by the hierarchy of thousands of shades of green. Surrounded by flying creatures, from butterflies to majestic birds, acquiescent in the element air, flowing in the air like stars dance in the sky. He closes his eyes; the reality reversal appears—breathing the violet connection to the Empyrean universe; the solid-silver mountains, reaching the edges of the multidimensional trance dance, visible in the reflection of the lake, now a ballet of symbols that all form the understanding of absoluteness.

Empyrean Universe

Reviewing reflection of the understanding
Devotion of the infinite existence
Enigmatic magnetic representation of time
Tears morphing into pearls, flowing
Wheeling into Consciousness of being luminary

Transcending the evolution of creation
Remembering the torch of illumination
Concluding silence of devotion, annex my
breath to the orchestra of evolution
embody the gravity

Blue marble in the gates of celestial realms
Angelic parade confused by river of pearls
Sounds of superlative melody in conjunction with
Vibration of the sonorous clarity submissive to the
Modulation within the transparent construction
of creation

> Member of the music in the cells
> Melody in the ecstasy of entity
> our experience of the Empyrean Universe written in
> the wishes
> Two hearts' desire, cross the silk road of reincarnation

Return to space in the current breath, inhaling gently; moving belly juicing the sequence of a union. Creating a being of tranquility, he is completed. Ready to continue the path toward the union. His beloved daydreamer manifested from particles of love.

The magician is traveling from his mountain home, a peaceful creation surrounded by utterly beautiful nature and vibrations of such an enormous penetration. The crystal caves and timeless arena he created there allows him to be present in multidimensional dimensions and keep attracting a fluent, eloquent understanding of the experiences he practices alone with occasional company.

Many Suns ago a calling came to him. Enter a timeline of sparkling tenderness. A mystery wrapped in ancient beauty, a voyage guided by the heart.

Today he is walking toward the annual meeting of the full Society of Atlantis, led by the highest priestess herself; all the members in the city states and temples will be present, active and nonactive. All master ranks and political heads.

Snow-Halo is a retired magician after leaving his title in one of the temples at a relatively young age, upon falling in love with his high-priestess teacher. However, Snow-Halo knew it was the last teaching she could give him. It guided him to a voyage of self-discovery and self-education. Eventually, he was given a position in a temple, but it was not calling him anymore.

"Remembering those times makes me smile, sweet adventures with her," Snow-Halo recalls. Those memories of walking with her in the thick forest are the reason for choosing this route. He enters the ancient temple and tries to solve the puzzle of the undisclosed backdoor.

"But that was another life, and without my epithet." He winks to himself and stands up. He has a violet robe, with decorated hood assigned penetrating rare-metal symbols; the rope shows signs of wear, carrying the music of life experiences, and so does his smile.

The route will take him across a densely flourishing forest.

As a magician, he shuffles through dimensions. At intervals he enters magical realms, sometimes for entertainment but mostly to make a connection. The origins of myths expressed in the Atlantean individual experience are usually in storytelling histories.

The stories illuminated eons ago in the Atlantean golden moments, and Snow-Halo was just a young apprentice in his first incarnation as a human being. This, he holds dear in his consciousness. He sinks into daydreaming and a desire from an earlier incarnation of his—sensing the spirit of humanity, a reminder by a curious whisperer from the beyond. Remembering can be a disappointment or a reawakened passion. Conceivably toward the new illumination.

"Dear forest near me, today I enter, and I wonder at your gift to me this time. I wonder why creatures have given you such names and so many stories transpire in you.

"I am yours to entertain." He concludes the intention and enters the forest as the violet fades in the colors of the woods.

The night sets down as the moon rises to its highest point and paints the silver shade. A soundless echo travels in space as the night-loving creatures blast into life. Glowing eyes appear in surroundings where the moon takes her steps. Breaths and stealth maneuvers are constantly present as wildlife plays and hunts. There are shadows in the dark, sounds in the depths, an ominous feeling someone is observing you.

The path travels across majestic trees; Snow-Halo's legs receive support from the stones laid down by previous generations.

The hidden, or a dark forest, a source of magical stories.

Not that it's not hard to find, its location camouflaged in the middle of Atlantis.

The prophecy was given several generations ago by a group of priestesses and priests—recorded in an ancient language and stored close to the Temple of Venus, underneath the seventh element. A crystal scroll was created; seven creatures protected it: five mortals, two gods; they vanished from Atlantis after the creation of the manuscript. Fractions of the script oozed into the ether, making the forest the hidden location of a grand illusion, where worlds collide.

"I cannot remember a more confusing conjunction and displacement of Atlantean energies. No one agrees anymore about the direction of this continent. I assume we have a good selection of New Age know-it-alls, ready to deliver a payload of disposable wisdom. Now when the new nanocomputer is set up, all connected to the CPU, we'll suddenly become superhuman. It will be very irritating to listen to—would love the humor— but it's not the time." Snow-Halo speaks with himself and adds a layer of preparation.

In a next step, he freezes in place. A massive magnetic energy blasts on top of him, up front in the azure, the impact powerful, magnetizing him in location; the bluish, static magnetic field generated by the object entering into this dimension provides no escape for him. He lets out a scream of agony as the electricity overwhelms his being. All is still or appears to be. Leaves are flying off the trees and falling upwards in a silent slow motion. As the source of the phenomenon opens into an immense tunnel, the ear-ringing explosion forces out a whipping wave of energy, knocking Snow-Halo onto a rock. He holds onto his consciousness and reaches into his pocket to find a crystal stone, his first stone, and holds it tight.

His eyes record the massive *Black Pyramid*, aka *Dark Pyramid*, making a pulsing noise as it passes him, then disappears out of his sight. He passes out.

CHAPTER 3

Snow-Halo is in the darkness of his consciousness, the depth of the coma released by the blast. Expression of time in the chronology of illusion, he is descending deeper in a blue-violet juncture of dimensions, the amplitude of the infinite escape. Rhyming beat of the electrical conjunction as rhythms of grand creation collapse in one word.

Reflection of the astral image projected into the reality of a parallel consciousness . . .

With a twist, shake, and a scream, Snow-Halo jumps up in a seated position.

Confusion gathers around as he views the reality around him. He is in control, yet still observing. Recognizing a new addition into this life. Sooner or later, perhaps not yet manifested, a stream of thought patterns or a dream, he feels as if he is guiding these new emotions forward.

He stands up, touches his body, and walks toward the mirror. A familiar reflection welcomes him. A man in the early part of his life experience, blessed with health and the ambition of creation.

He touches his cheek, feeling the face to be true. "Not an illusion." He waits for the answer. No response echoes. The steps of a horse in the distance are reverberating towards him. Turning to face the beam of the sound, he views a woman riding a black horse through a green garden.

Towards a little cabin, an open window the single glazed, dimmed relic; the paintwork faded in time, curtain flapping in the wind, singing the last goodbyes. Is it a past life so rustic or decayed into an uncomplicated experience? A puzzle begins.

A warm, tender feeling builds in his heart and bursts into an enigmatic explosion as she descends from her horse with such artistic competence; it's as if she were a ballet dancer. Only in his heart.

He sits in the confusion of a lifetime. With reality not opened up to him quite yet, his questions rise into the air like steam. The space between truth and illusion fades willingly. This is Snow-Halo's inexplicable testimony of attraction.

He focuses quickly on his hand, pointing it at the open window in which his beauty awaits him, and tries to close it. "Nothing happened!" He glares with bewilderment at his palms, does a quick read of his lines, and realizes that for the time being, this magic has settled into his life.

"Honey, join me in the garden. I made us breakfast; you will love it."

A stream of words in a language unfamiliar, yet understandable.

"*Oui*" spits off his tongue in an embarrassing attempt to communicate with her. The conflict produces a strange stream of emotions, a problem to reflect on during hurricane rages inside. "There are no answers for my questions; I'm either in a dream or have woken into a fantasy novel."

Snow-Halo dresses, noticing that there is not much he can do now; either way, this experience is his present reality. Wearing clothes seems to be very complicated, doors are thin and insignificant without symbols. The body is slow and tense; yet inside he feels explosive. *Is this an extreme experiment perhaps, or the deepest fear I carry?*

Another question arises and no one can answer.

He walks toward the slowly appearing door, observing mystical objects in the house and their simplicity in the clutter around them. These things are not of his reality.

As he places his hand on the doorknob, a *click* sounds. He is struck with a sudden feeling of autonomous body awareness.

The brightness of the day is blinding for a moment, a reaction he could not expect. Unable to follow a spectrum of the energies in the stream of sunlight unknown to him, until now.

He takes wobbling steps towards the garden, decorated with the arrangement of flowers and a pond of water. In the middle stands a half-full table and a woman placing seemingly dull knives next to the plate. He wonders about the practice here. She turns toward him and smiles. This moment confuses the thought patterns inside him, and they're replaced by a desire, the meteoric need for ecstasy. His mind rushes with a sharp, volcanic feeling.

Snow-Halo would like to walk straight toward the woman, but something tells him to hold off for now and observe. So he walks toward her and allows flow to appear.

"Mon Amour" is directed with such warmth and compassion towards him, he has to hold his heart to avoid exploding in this instant.

The follow-up is a gentle, soft kiss on the lips, leaving him to, just and only, hold his body functions in the behavior expected if remaining in the realms of the ordinary. The twitching limbs, beating heart, running blood. Luckily his sense of smell started to pick up the scent emanating from the table, an assortment of substances he cannot recognize; a blindness to this knowledge does not dampen his appetite. Gently flow, relax and seemingly his body can fill the sensation of the nerves in him; this distraction is not sufficient to take his focus off the woman opposite him and the pleasure he gets in seeing her shovel food into her mouth.

"My love, everything good with you today? You are acting a bit slow today?" She smiles, with a big giggle.

Snow-Halo would like to ask many questions, knowing he cannot actually—not to make everything even more confused.

"Yes, my love, all is good today. Just crowded in my head, I'll soon be okay. How was the morning horseback ride?"

"Just fine, I went riding near the lake and met our neighbor Daniel; he was also there with his horse!"

Snow-Halo is shocked by the sudden formation of nasty feelings and catches himself thinking dark things about Daniel. He feels immediate urges to carry his woman into the house and hide her from all who dare see her. His jealous emotions prompt him to ask, "Why do I do not have a horse?" More questions streamline themselves to him. Naturally, the noises emanating from his newfound jealousy add flavor to his questioning of this reality.

He acknowledges that if he moves on in this burden of unfinished emotions, he could repeat his lessons again. Morning transfers into day, and evening soon makes its way as they sit on the terrace, watching the Sun travel over the horizon.

He has held on; he waited for all to align in the *for so long* to complete his cycle. To experience a pure moment in life. To all of the questions he asked, the answer is next to him. The smooth silky skin, sparkling eyes, and the tender twist in her smile as she rattles off bubbly words. Lust of love could be yours.

She turns her head, and his focus shifts to her lips. His hand tenderly moves under her skirt. The pulsating heartbeat, the connection unexplainable. The final loss of any reality existing outside of her. The passion expanding the carnal desire. The capitulation of animal instinct.

CHAPTER 4

A monumental golden pillar rises above the horizon, sunrays reflecting off its surface as a beacon of enigmatic, dreamlike hallucination. Sunrays welcomed and reflected in a hypnagogic orchestra of celestial dance; a symphony of dreamy light. Each carving reflecting a shimmering crystal spectrum; an emblem of a heavenly rainbow. Synergy bred inside the passion of ruby and the glitter of sapphire. Clustering in the space stands a stage under the Sun and stars. The highest bar in the consciousness of Atlantis; surreal experience perishes in the waves of the golden cloud of magic.

In the center stands a woman who welcomes the rhythmic conjunction of space and moment, her arms spread to the wind as her white dress mimics the movement of the ocean waves. The breath an interval of ethereal communication, transmission of exhaling and inhaling transparent intelligence. A mediation of harmony in the balance of this voyage. "Envision the abstract painting of a confused unicorn in the wheels of time."

She breathes, she listens, she feels: knowing her faith is about to change. She stands up and walks gently toward the entrance; the movement of her female figure captures the imagination of the gods as her body drops a perfect shadow in all corners of the stage.

Her name is Mirabella. She is a priestess in the Temple of Venus.

Mirabella enters the temple. Gentle harmonic sounds ring as she passes the resonance field, allowing her to access the interior halls. She enters and is welcomed by twenty priestesses. Holding their crystals close, they hum an angelic hymn as she passes by. Typically, a source of plasma is created within this practice, and while she walks by, Mirabella remembers her avatar experience with great joy. She gives them a warm smile and enters into her chamber.

A chamber of a beautiful stillness resonating a purple light of harmony.

Perfectly sized, flowing round a catacomb. A view is opening into a serene panorama, taking the breath away. Mirabella opens a knot in her dress, letting it gently drift down on her skin as gravity tows the dress toward the floor; her skin welcomes the space. She grabs a scarf-like fabric and gently covers her hips, allowing poetry to rebound.

Moving to the alcove of her sacred objects, she gathers them with dignity, knowing it's time to depart, for now. Mirabella knows she can take only what she will be needing, so each item is selected with careful intuition. Once ready, she enters her wardrobe. "A dark red dress will do," she feels, and dresses her body. She slips a dagger into her belt, together with other objects she has gathered. Mirabella is ready. Leaving her chamber, she encounters all twenty-two priestesses in the hallway.

"Sisters, I must depart for an exploit, for my heart has shown me a calling. Through the passing time, my soul has yearned for a creation unknown. I feel this desire in my visions as I move into new dimensions. I shall return, a new woman," she informs the receptive group of young ladies.

"I am going toward the sound I hear. Toward blood in my veins.

"I thank you, my sisters, for holding space for me. For my growth, joy, and tears on the path of the priestess. The temple will always carry my presence." Mirabella speaks with trembling voice and drops a tear onto the floor; her memories of love and relationship with them marks the best time of her life. Now she needs to follow her heart, even if it hurts.

Mirabella steps forward, eying the crystal mirror, and smiles to herself. Moving her curly long blonde hair and staring at her green eyes, she nods to herself as if signing a contract.

She runs along the pillar. The temple of Venus is atop the clouds, its foundation created by a unique microclimate She clutches the post that she must jump down from.

"It's a long fall, many heartbeats," she thinks and contemplates the idea of going into a teleportation crystal.

"That would not be such a cinematic exit, and my sisters are watching, possibly questioning my commitment." Mirabella runs through her options quickly and reminds herself that she has done this once before. "The jump must be perfect," she thinks. There is a railing halfway down the drop, which works as a transport device and shall carry her where her heart desires. "Let's go!" She takes a deep breath and jumps. The blood starts running in her body as she descends toward an unknown destiny. Mirabella screams inside.

"Fear perhaps, scared a bit, but trust, YES!" She allows her body to work, the winds pushing her toward the active ring.

The ring appears as a small point below, and in a heartbeat she is in the middle of it. Just a fraction of a blink, and she is away.

Snow-Halo opens his eyes—awakened by the scream of a woman, answered with a scream of his own. He spent the night unconscious of this realm. And as he wakes, pain informs him of his presence as his consciousness and self-awareness come alive again. Intense pain in every cell forms in him. It's not just physical pain, the blast and energies of his cell communication—a trauma in the making. He gets the body responding one atom at the time. He musters his courage and pulls his body into a seated position, despite the crippling pain of each cell's displacement. From this point, he is able to grab his valuables and start healing himself.

"I'm not in any condition to walk much more; better to head into the temple." Snow-Halo sighs and replays the accident in his crystals and grabs his healing potion. "I'm a short distance from the ancient ruins and lake; it will cause a great deal of discomfort to go there again. But the best option is to go and heal. I cannot activate the beacon, as last night's crew might be close." Snow-Halo goes over his options.

Emotions run him down. He would not like to return to the ruins, not after what happened before.

There is a valid reason that he is still alive. "Remarkably viable," Snow-Halo repeats while taking slow and painful steps towards the ancient temple.

CHAPTER 5

Tranquility in an abandoned underground dome. An ambiance of humidity and darkness serves as the stage. Eerie patterns of the past centuries echo in the silent walls. The trapped energies of ancient practices perfected in the past. The atmosphere changes as Mirabella splashes into the watery pool, accompanied by her long, multidimensional scream let out upon entering this reality. Sinking deeper toward the center of the inner Earth.

"When will this diving end?" Mirabella asks herself with slight concern in her voice.

Eventually, her body comes to a halt. "Much better. Just darkness in all corners . . . *up* is there? Or *down* is up? Even up is down; should I go down . . . ?" Mirabella is mumbling in her head, trying to find direction while feeling her body's need for oxygen. Her body floats in the direction of the ground. Is it gravity that pulls her? Finally, she reaches the surface. "Ah, I can breathe this pleasant air deep into my lungs." She enjoys the inhale, only to find a damp, mildly unattractive scent creeping into her nose. Her face expresses unfamiliar emotions, something she is not used to. Hair dangles toward her hips as Mirabella rises out of the water.

She opens her travel bag, thanking herself for not taking a heavy load. Gently sweeping over the crystal, she observes it in full light as it shines in all its brilliance. The light and warmth enter simultaneously in the space around her. Mirabella slowly walks toward the red glass in the wall that seems to be resonating with her personal stone. She hangs up her clothes and walks naked toward two doors. One door has a symbol of stars; the other, planets and moons. "There should be only one door . . . But two?" She winces, hoping this is not one of the labyrinth temples, where a stream of choices is presented leading to a subconscious timeline of decisions.

"My lovely heart, do we go for the planet and moons?" she asks her inner self in mild concern, as a choice feels imminent. "The silver moon has never disappointed me." She nods to herself and gives it a push. The chosen door opens, with determination, to a gallery of confusion. "An octagon-shaped room? The ancients used this in their lost ceremonies." She breathes, knowing her knowledge ends here. Now, her soul is in charge to find the next clue. Mirabella stands stranded, focusing on the challenge as the door behind her closes and locks. Gently, she looks behind, knowing her past lies there, enclosed in the room of energies. History is written off as her crystal shuts down.

Moonlight appears as a silver string of the divine ray emanating in the center of the octagon.

"Moonlight?" Mirabella is baffled at how it's been captured here. The light is ecstatic, alive and electric. It calls her to come closer.

In an instant, she feels a piano playing in her heart, a tender song of love; she envisions a ray from the moon formed ages ago. Something beautiful, old. The substance of adornment to capture in her deep, beautiful smile. Her third floor of love, now digesting the capsule of excitement.

The comforting embrace lasts as time pauses. She experiences an alluring essence; the romance of lovers' walks on silver-shaded bridges, the poetry of a butterfly's flight. Mirabella holds her heart, keeping her love inside as her heart pumps and beats. A childlike smile shines on her smooth face as she feels her love song radiate. She faints onto the floor.

Falling into a trance of both confusion and clarity, Mirabella leaves her body. She ascends into a surreal reality, viewing her unconscious self lying on the ground as she spirals up toward space—having a priestess's faith in the process. Countless times, Mirabella has done this consciously. Her consciousness feels a strong pull toward a particular point in the universal reality. Responding to the guidance from where her journey pulls her, she reaches a gate guarded by the breath of dragons and the power of lions. Mirabella feels the atoms colliding in this space. She sings the hymn of its energy. In this moment, the essence of her voyage is exposed.

"Welcome," voices echo in her being. A transcending vibration reflects all of the dimensions she currently occupies.

"Thank you. May I request your presence?" she replies in a soft voice and observes her surroundings in this celestial home . . . a paradise, she feels.

She views the construction of rainbow vortexes, surrounded by waterfalls of golden water. She admires the sparks of pulsar stars and guides her view outside, to the slope this palace hovers on.

"Come in. I am waiting for you," the voice says softly. Mirabella hesitates a moment, then starts to flow toward huge golden doors that open into a great hallway. She can see a woman sitting on her throne.

White long hair descends down the stairs, her ensemble made of silver, shimmering needles of light.

Mirabella feels small in her presence, yet bravely holds her space.

"What I am looking at?" she questions.

"I am Allura, a sunray, blanketed in the stardust of gravity. An angel in the core; a being from the ancient race. I am the source of your experience here. I invited you to visit me the time you fell down into the stars." Allura smiles, making Mirabella more relaxed.

Allura continues, "As you must notice, your voice is here. I will give reason to the questions you ask. You will become a mother soon, to a dear soul for us. My summoning you is connected. We in Atlantis walk in menace. Our collective souls will trigger energies and guidance in the temples. The ancients will return."

Mirabella stands like a statue, her hands holding her belly while looking at the clear manifestation of her body. "A child?" Her jaw expands like a python's. "With whom? Will there be an entrance of a particular soul into my life?" she asked while thinking, "Not the priest who keeps cementing his energies to mine." Her eyes widen as she projects the future in front of her in horror.

"Your souls will unite at the right time. This moment will come. I will guide you into the sarcophagus to rest while the movement of energies takes place," Allura replies.

She listens to the instructions in the stillness and weighs the news delivered to her. "It cannot be that priest. He surely wants to impregnate me. Our souls would be forever one! What misery! Uniting the priest-and-priestess classes would surely follow on this . . . what will come of it all?" Mirabella trembles at the idea of putting her unique vibes in danger. Placing her head on the pillow, she lays her body inside the sarcophagus. Allura looks at Mirabella with her round, golden eyes and smiles. "I have a better plan for you than the creepy priest . . ." She winks and closes the cover.

Mirabella closes her eyes and feels the shock of her lifetime; a lightning bolt inside the sarcophagus takes her to the next phase.

CHAPTER 6

Snow-Halo arrives at the temple of the ancients. The trek he undertook is accompanied by aches and cramps. He stops before entering the sacred space. He views the site as a sanctuary he could never ultimately incorporate. Knowing the place, location, and the energies would be a turning point in his soul. Eventually he will submit and move away from the sphere of these powers. The sacrifice that occurred here is left in the dark. His understanding forgotten in the loneliness of a single room.

His light-blue eyes reflect the architecture before him as his heart beats like a drunken drum. The design of the temple is ageless—the stillness of balance, in harmony with nature. The lack of worship and absence of humans are noticeable; yet life has preserved the location exactly.

Integrated next to the bluest, deepest pond he has ever laid eyes on, he notices that the lake represents a perfect circle, protected by the hilltops and large trees. The temple opens into an enigmatic synergy; a detailed fabric of construction. Inside the beautiful pillars, it enjoys vast vegetation and the might of the stone/crystal material it is built on. The walls, roof, and floor covered with written language; still a mystery. Incredibly forgotten: framed by extraordinary beings of Atlantis hundreds of thousands of years ago, it holds secrets that neither masters nor any other class in current Atlantis could interpret. The former temple was occupied by a clan of magicians and priestesses spanning extensive periods of time. The objective: to retrieve the lunar and solar information, emerging in the reflection of the temple walls. Despite using modern technology and wisdom gathered from the ancient scriptures, nevertheless, the study failed.

Reflections of memories: the operating time in the temple, synergy of the voyage, the collaboration of hearts. The ancient pathways hold wisdom acquired through the cosmic connection. Capturing images of the mystery, haunted clues in the darkness.

An embrace in search of a moment. The appearance of an angelic octave; the soft, vibrant flow of the mountain song:

> *Harmony in my synergy, symphony in the symbols. The knot tied on my universe loosens to expand the life I have. The rhythm of the celestial heartbeat is repeating. The glorious fusion of creation, desire, and longing. Tender tear in the space of iris, tear of Venus rotating the wheel of my life.*

"When I left the temple in the past, I promised to never return. I did not want to explore anymore; yet you called me back. Do you have an answer to my question? I ask, as I am here now before you." Snow-Halo awakens the salted wounds inside him. He takes short steps toward the entrance—a mystifying experience as the field of energy is electrified. The thrilling sensation passes through each molecule traveling with him, penetrating each atom entering this space. He places his hand on one of the pillars near the main entrance, knowingly allowing the temple to amplify the process of healing. Shivers of pulses entering in a beat of a heart and imagination of each conscious spark of life extracts the transcended spark of the curing spirit.

He continues toward the temple, stopping at the entrance—the central carving allowing memories to surface, back to a time when he came here with his teacher, a high priestess. He can still feel the younger version of himself standing for the first time to observe a show that was out of this world. Watching the moonlight dance with the sunrays. A hologram created from the starlight. "Testimony left behind for both of us," he thinks silently and continues deeper in the vault. While he strolls forward, his fingertips are touching the symbols on the walls; each time a small charge of electric energy triggered. Symbols are resonating with the energies he holds, an exchange of information created at the moment the touch manifests. He only guesses by the feeling—the communication nonverbal, but emotional and angelic by nature. The only clue left behind is the stream of sounds filling the transcending path to the central chamber, forming a musical symphony of inner being. What he is and what he could be.

"Surface of the soul," he says and focuses on the central chamber.

In the dazzling stream of moonlight, he steps into the chamber. It's a circular room, deep underground. An octave of an angelic hymn plays there, its echo everlasting in the allure of the house of mystery. A dome opens toward the stars, beckoning the light to shine on this careful design where each ray compliments the mystery left behind by the ancients. The room is thirteen levels deep, level after level taking him down to the golden crystal ball. In return, the ball collects the light and shimmers its chosen symbols at that moment. The dance and movement of the symbols are more than hypnotic.

"It's my turn to view this show." Snow-Halo focuses his attention and creates a soft place for himself.

I traveled and failed
Asked the questions, where there are no answers
In the starlight stood alone
Tested by time

Rusted my heart became
Standing nowhere in the starlight
Conscious of the conclusion
I am asking for one more destiny

Tear froze in the ice cube
below the plains of Antarctica, perhaps
Release the rust, whisper a heartbeat
I scream one more faith

The ecstasy of ocean
Beginning of the hallucination
Reverie of the dreamlike creation
Testimony of moon dust

Why do questions, in years, realize the answers
Anytime the tender starlight travels in the Earth
Asking *why* the moonlight is trapped in the cave
The hallucination of the dream

CHAPTER 7

An earthquake-like vibration travels through Mirabella when her consciousness returns. Her shivering body is resting on a cold, wet stone floor. Her inhalation is rapid and profound. The experiences in the last day have overwhelmed her etheric and physical energies. "What is going on?" She requests an answer. "My heart so soft and safe, mind escaped far away, yet why am I still in this cold place? The voyage I've entered into has led me here." Mirabella puts her hand on her heart and cannot hold in her cries. Her emotions and feelings are explosive. Her heart is unusually bright, enlarged and magical. Her reflections bonding with her tranquil magic. "I am not going to stay here for a heartbeat. I am finding my way out immediately!" She realizes this clearly and stands up. With trembling legs and tremulous arms, Mirabella starts to center herself. Breathing fire inside, she activates a life force and in no time at all enjoys the waves of heat traveling in her body, heart breathing, leveling, and her core centering. "Now, my eyes, let's get this same clarity in the darkness." She amplifies her focus to view energies in the darkness.

Once the spectrum of astral reflections is visible, Mirabella can navigate nearly as well as in the daylight.

"This is the room I first appeared in. I expect it doesn't have doors anymore. It's a completely sealed, round room with a high roof and pool in the middle. I cannot see any energy exits either." She ponders her options, her eyes focused on the water, watching its movement and observing the broad chromatic scale of energies.

"The pool—could it be the exit? It's deep, perhaps bottomless." Mirabella weighs her next move, gently biting her lips as thoughts of the last voyage start to present themselves in her mind.

Sure, when entering the priesthood, sacrifices are along the path. "The priest will be plaster to my crystals! Is my choice to stay forever in this room or embark on a journey with him? Is this the universe's way to firmly guide me toward this destiny?" Mirabella nibbles her nails as the moment of choice draws closer.

"Union? Indeed, I cannot feel him. I only feel my heart beating so gently. Is it something fresh coming to me?" Mirabella reflected back on the old forecast of her destiny. In her childhood, she had seen a vision of her and this priest together. She liked him as a child, but the current version does not please her.

"My legacy will not be a pile of bones in this corner. For sure, if my heart gives me the challenge to expand, I will take it as always. Who knows where it leads, whom I'm dealt by my eternal soul?" She confirms her decision to enter into the water. Mirabella stands on the ring surrounding the well, gazing into the energies of turquoise spiraling toward the white center in the shimmering water. Confident in knowing the route out, she focuses on her breath and ties her belongings around her waist. "Become a priestess, attach these heavy objects onto your hips and jump into the bottomless well. Yes, this is my life!" she babbles, placing her fingers on her nose, giving a good squeeze while jumping in the air—compassionately understanding that destiny is not in her hands anymore. She bounces against the watery surface, detecting how long to stall before breaking further into the watery element. Once again cold water travels upward through her body as she slowly descends towards the endless bottom. Surrounded by cold darkness, Mirabella relaxes her body, places her hands in the center of her heart, and lets everything go.

Snow-Halo opens his eyes with the gentle assistance of the emerging Sun. Outlines of butterflies shadow and circle the lake. All night had been dedicated to the practice of healing. Meeting the morning Sun after the night's starlight. Hiding the breath of dream, a seed of secret imagination. He had a fantasy of the beloved vision quest; a leap into the lunatic seduction forecast in the daydream.

> *Birth the fire in the darkest pit; then take the heat from her breath,*
> *close the eyes, feel the movement, the fever of the desire.*
> *Inhale the flavor deep, in essence, shower in the drops of salt.*
> *Temper the temptation, grant the fire entry, bless the light.*
> *In the dark, follow the heat in the heart.*
> *Feel the beat in the tempo, hold the pace of the heart.*
> *Bend the curvature of Earth, blessed goddess in her; blow on her fire.*
> *See the shadow of the light, let the heart undress her hips.*
> *Breathe.*

"If I were to depart in this moment, I would arrive at the second day of the gathering in the Capitol. A lovely contest of the leading figures, expressing different aspects and perspectives of life. Entering into the amusing arena of debate, where individuals from remote corners, with simple ideas, collide in front of her majesty; the screams echoing deep into the dimensions." Snow-Halo is laughing, remembering the jokes of previous years. He is happy, as his health and energies provide him with full enjoyment.

"The lake seems so tempting for an excellent swim or dive. I haven't seen it this turquoise before." Snow-Halo stops for a hypnotic moment and makes an instant decision to jump in.

As his body slingshots into the air, leaving his clothes behind, time seems to stall. Soft amazement travels across his body as a flicker of reality starts to materialize, and reality appears to slow down.

The scene is now set at night; today's greeting was by the Sun alone. Unity of souls in flames created by the beginning of a fire. In the shyness of a dreamlike cosmic dance, he receives evanescent memories of a velour voice. The spirit Bianca's blessing emerges from the stars—a soul of a pulsar a rotating neutron star, remnants of a long since exploded supernova. The active taste of a lover's lips, in a paradigm of trance. Perfume of feminine drops of tenderness. Her devotion like the aroma of a butterfly. The glitter of stars in her eyes traveling across generations as informal love letters.

Words whispered by the lake, a selected few drops on the surface. Gently, as fluently as a flute played in the harmony of nature.

The outcome of the diary written by a feather pen, ink and breath dried out. Today's book was written, a chapter addressed by the grace of the soul, in breath arrived with rays of the Sun. Say no more; just trace the aroma of devotion.

CHAPTER 8

Qali is striking an authoritative pose. His eyes reflect exhaustion while remaining focused on the details before him. He is in the operating room of the *Black Pyramid*, the command center. Each time relocation is ordered, the experienced crew establishes a joint direction of forced energy. This guides the ship's computer to the desired location. It's a task of focusing collective energies into the ship's guiding system, which in return charges the dimensional crystals resonating with the aimed location.

The operating room is a multidimensional hexagram. In its center is the glass computer. Its corners have room for a manned operator, tasked to adjust aspects of vibration, dimension, and direction of the time and movement of the physical temple.

"Located! Reading coordinates. They are showing us deep inside of the dark forest's lake. Prepare for the final phase. Return to your workstations and access the mainframe."

The commanding voice echoes in the operating room as Qali passes the sharp message to the operators.

Qali has another name: Project Alpha. In the early parts of his life, he was an outcast, a talented trickster lurking in the corners of the Capitol. A child of a priest and a political figure, abandoned by his parents at an early age, he was left to wander in the intersections of possible outcomes.

At this time the immortal Black Queen offered him a role, in the aftermath of his attempt to steal her belongings. At first, she thought to punish him, but after a careful DNA screening in which she discovered his bloodline, she revised her plan, and devised Project Alpha—emergent in the beam of transcendental technology, fired into his DNA.

Now, after genetic mutations ordered by the Queen, he stands as Qali, though traces of his past identity remain.

Because of his bloodline and training acquired in the temples back home, Qali has a higher perspective compared to the other project beings. As the first "creation" of the Queen, he was given advanced crystal implants in his bloodstream. She also had an inner dimensional being embedded inside him, something Qali would like to remove from his energies.

Topping off the love the Queen had for her creation, Qali went through extensive DNA modifications granting him a useful set of powers. This came at a significant cost, the need to inject a serum into his bloodstream to keep his cellular construction in place.

When this injection is needed, the metallic, harmonic voice appears in his mind, screaming:

ACTION IMPLEMENT, MERGE, RESONATE.

The computed voice informs the crew of the task they must undertake. A new dimension of the grand plan has been unlocked for all. Qali feels a thrill rising up his spine.

With this excitement in his energies, Qali moves rapidly into his laboratory, carefully inspecting the workstation and the creature left in charge of the experimental substance. He eyes the holographic diameters.

"All balanced and in perfect positions. Prepare the human experiment, Delta! Proceed immediately," Qali commands the being. His mind starts to run through outcomes of the research (all theoretical up to this point).

"There is no room for error."

Time is of the essence. To execute this correctly, we need a test-subject human. The outcome cannot be authenticated if there is an access limit reserved for further calibration.

"I'll create one more simulation before testing it, in case all goes wrong. Get the human in the chamber and prepare the injections!" Kali commands Project Delta. He moves to his interface and activates the crystal computer, so that the equipment runs a series of security checks to clear access to the mainframe. In one thought, Qali has a direct link to the primary core of the *Black Pyramid*.

Focusing, he allows the computer to import necessary data to the frame; the result will be downloaded back to him. Reducing the risk of possible malfunction in his proceedings, he repeats this multiple times.

"Oh, the ecstasy experienced when connecting to the main grid." Qali contemplates it while downloading energy patterns. Connecting to the main network allows a symbiotic relationship with the *Black Pyramid*. It's deliberately designed to function like a highly addictive drug, giving an intense sensation of invisibility and physical satisfaction. Aside from energetic sensations, this euphoric connection allows management of the monitored cabal workforce and uploads their latest thought processes to the connected being.

Qali recognizes the network deep within himself, and the day seems to bring much pleasure. He understands the new unlocked dimension is something he has been waiting for. The surge of energies is massive and allows him to slightly levitate off the floor.

"Monumental energy, the sweet nectar of invincibility," he says, feeling stronger and more powerful than ever.-

His mind seems to be escaping deeper into the depths of the grid. Surreal sounds amplify in his mind, while his vision darkens by the moment.

"Death, darkness, and suffering. Rivers of blood filling the streets; insects covering the Sun; fire, rapes, and captured souls locked in the forever-lasting cycle of the prison of the mind and reincarnation. Jailed in nonfunctioning bodies with limited lifespans. Starvation, thirst, fear, maggots feasting on the body's consciousness while its soul is harvested by the cabal.

"Standing tall in front is the figure of the Black Queen; behind her stand the bloodthirsty elite, an army of cyborgs. Man and machine connected to the grid, her supercomputer updating their heartbeats, a black rain washing the cyborg contingent. The contingent next to its Queen. With a dagger in hand, she cuts me open, feasting on my blood. Her tongue split into two eyes, dark as charcoal; in her terror, one word written, a word I remember from my early years!"

Qali is shaken up so deeply that the connection breaks and he drops to the floor, lifeless, bleeding through the pores of his skin.

Project Delta processes the situation and moves to grab the serum injection Qali uses twice a day, injecting a third dose. Qali starts to show signs of life, twitching, moaning and eventually moving. He opens his eyes, only to see darkness everywhere.

"Delta, give me another dose. My implants are not attaching in my bloodstream correctly!" he shouts, with a shrill panic in his voice, while thinking of the destiny he has signed up for.

CHAPTER 9

Snow-Halo descends from the temple roof—his eyes reflecting the turquoise of the water. Pulses of mild curiosity and attraction amplify his voyage to the surface of the water. His eyes focus more deeply on the poetry of the lake. It calls to him and whispers of the existential dimensions existing in its depths. Something extraordinary is surfacing. And time enters in the stillness His hypnotic gaze focuses on his reflection, created by the lake. Integration of desire appearing.

Pleasant wind flows quietly.

A melody of friendship and love resonates in his heart.

Careless whispers in the wind sound like the voice of a lover in a hallowed union.

A gentle hum passes through each ear.

A slow spark of the past gone by, and with it, a tender teardrop falls.

Paused for a moment in the poetry of life, he inhales the magic, expecting truth to emerge in the solid beat of his heart.

Snow-Halo gently rubs his elements together, hoping to feel the spark leading toward an answer. His heart recognizes this poetry.

"The turquoise poem of a lifetime's scope of expression, anticipated in the unpredictable experience of unfolding, the essence of the communication of nature, the painting of poetry, an original artist of life?" Snow-Halo mutters while connecting to the nature surrounding him. Pictures evolve inside small waterdrops, and shades of images in the transient movement of the lake draw dancing pictures as the surface transforms into a silver theatre screen for him. The collection of memories hidden in the crystal consciousness is released by the union of separated energies.

He touches upon his inbreath, as when reversing the exhalation—an enigmatic calling to dive deep. Curving his body in the infinite moment of the movement expressing the desire to explore. Exemption of gravity from eternity; at least, he feels like it when sliding across the air. When his fingertips penetrate the water's surface, his vision drags him back from his past life. The cycle has ended.

"My first incarnation. In the distant future, tens of thousands of years ago. The ceremony of a soul in a fresh human experience. The reality of space travel. Seductive, unimaginable technological developments, coupled with unnatural lifespan and spiritual understanding of the mind/body/spirit complex. To be part of the devoted and elegant human being, the experience should have been beautiful."

It was not. In the incarnation he felt something inexplicable. A sensation of missing something. A gentle longing for something time and time again. Those sparks arose, and the quality of the emotions was so different. They had been gently rubbed away by the social and technological environment. Laws and systems made sure that partnerships and life would evolve without deep emotions, while genetics took the lead in the area of breeding. It was a clinically operated death of magic, love, and romance.

In the future, a metallic coldness would suffocate even the smallest spark of emotion. It would chill these feelings from the bloodstream to the soul. Yet though they were restrained and frozen, they existed still.

One day he would explore these forbidden aspects of human nature. A spark would ignite a passionate love affair, one that could only be sustained in a place like Atlantis, where love and magic still existed. The sensations of fingertips in motion and the silky, smooth skin of his future lover would cast a spell, traveling in the blink of an eye, and he would fall in love for the very first time. Snow-Halo has penetrated the surface of the deep blue lake, diving further into the abyss, guided by turquoise pulses. His eyes allow the darkness of the water to overrule them. He is ignorant of the depths of the water; yet he does not mind, as his physical senses are moot to him now. He relies on his heart to guide his path.

He is submerged in his own consciousness. His voyage is guided further down into the lake. As he searches for the purpose of his dive, his lungs burn and scream for oxygen. He ignores the physical sensations, focusing on the flow of water surrounding his aura. His pulse slows as he recognizes a golden light shimmering nearby. The shimmer is reflected from long blonde hair dancing in the water by his side. A female body is floating in the lake's slow current, carried unconsciously through the blue abyss. Snow-Halo feels her energy and ponders her presence here next to him. He snaps back quickly and recognizes the danger of staying underwater with her for too long. He swims toward her and holds her in his arms. He pushes against the bottom of the lake's floor, and a heavy bag of crystals drops from her hand as they rocket toward the surface.

"Priestesses and their modern needs . . . Those portable ceremony items were only weighing her down, keeping her from floating to the surface," Snow-Halo thinks to himself as he swims toward the top of the water. As they move closer to the surface, his vision is still clouded, allowing him to see only a dark picture of the scenery above him. He wishes to see her face, as he can discern that she is beautiful, and it would give him great feelings of joy to view her. They rise up gently as feathers would glide through the wind. His body screams in pain, his lungs gasping for air, while her body is still but alive. No movement comes from her. Together they reach the world above this watery chamber. Sunlight pours over Snow-Halo's face as he breathes the pure air and sets his eyes on her.

CHAPTER 10

" The chairman of the independent temples is a threat to us. Once her leadership is removed, we will unite in the new Atlantis."

A holographic metallic voice echoes from a red crystal-like object rays of light that have formed the shape of a human. The person projecting himself from the crystal is Commander Alfa. This display has not only allowed his presence in the form of light, but also allows him to touch and see as if he were there in reality.

"Commander Alfa, are you are proposing we eliminate her?" a man replies. The man is titled Mr. Prime Selected. A timid man with postwar scars as a testimony to support his weariness.

Mr. Prime Selected is a being outside of all current powers; in the play, he is partly dead, partly alive.

His scars express the horrors of the last war, an existing testimony of death.

He is sitting comfortably in his cathedral-type chair, a biocybernetic uniform holding his human form in this reality—unable to restore, regenerate, his cells due to the offensive bioweapon used in the final days of the last war.

The alien technology preserves his condition, his form transparent and liquid as a result of the unique treatments. The atmosphere around him is hazy, cold, metallic. At times he resides in other dimensions. Half dead, half alive. His eye contact feared by the people of Atlantis, a fiery gateway to darkness.

"Our team of scientists confirmed that the ancient dome is exactly where you thought, and we know it's possible to activate the dome again as informed. It would give us the power to rule over Atlantis."

Silence fills the room while Mr. Prime Selected stares at the beautiful view outside. A great lake lined with colorful gardens opening up toward the mountains.

"Commander Alfa, you know my ship crashed in this lake that we now view. I saw my crew, my colleagues, disintegrate instantly. I often wonder why I was the only survivor. I believe the experiments we were conducting at the ancient sites saved me and altered my DNA, made it strong enough to defend me from the virus, me alone."

"We thought our cause to be valiant. Did we not design a better world after the war? The population was severely damaged, our government weakened. Atlantis had deserted its values, and altercations between ruling parties broke out. The Queen would never approve elimination of the chairman. Perhaps it won't be necessary, once the dome is activated again," says Commander Alfa.

"Enter the site and prepare to enable the dome. The control panel and energy source are not far from the entrance. Our instruments will pick up their radiation signals, and we will be able to track their underground location. We will use our tools to manipulate any locked doors, and your cruiser shield will protect you from attacks. However, you should prepare for some casualties," Prime Selected informs those present.

"Mr. Prime Selected, what should we do regarding the Black Temple?"

"Nothing. The renegade group is not our problem at this time!"

Mr. Prime Selected walks away, entering into a hall nearby, with high ceilings and black marble. He stands a moment and feels the energy of the hall. He focuses on the destination desired as blue mist appears. His body is diluted into the cloud and he vanishes.

He travels far across the plains and lands in the mountains—arriving in a hall projecting golden beams of light from every angle. He heads up the stairway that appears before him. A sense of serenity washes over him. He reaches the top and pushes open a great door, of overwhelming size and weight.

"Ancients and their passion for large doors," Mr. Prime Selected thinks while passing, and gives a cheeky smile.

"Mr. Prime Selected, what are you doing here? You know this temple is sacred and not to be entered." An older female figure walks toward him. She approaches him with a magnetic self-confidence, gracefully wearing a black-and-gold dress on her body.

She is Abyss, holder of ancient knowledge

"Can we drop the titles? I came here to offer you a new timeline, something that even you cannot refuse, Abyss." Mr. Prime Selected is piercing in his message and takes one step closer.

"Devon, I am all ears. Isn't that a fantasy of yours?" Abyss asks, stepping toward the windows of the room—observing the mountains reflecting into the white walls of the cube, each wall holding a beautiful view of the kingdom she rules. Her cube was simple, just a red carpet in the middle and a black crystal desk next to it; within the corners of the cube a gentle fire was dancing, warming the space.

To her, Devon Prime Selected was always a mystery. It's practically impossible for another life form to enter the temple in which she resides. Even highly trained priests, priestesses, and magicians have met their obstacles. She questioned Devon's talents. He had never held a position of mystical power. His DNA was warped at the ancient sites and again in the crash. Instead of the war weapons demolishing his body, they triggered yet another disfiguration in his molecular structure, making him even more powerful than before. She had not chosen to question him about his journey to mystical power. Strange things were normal in Atlantis nowadays. Confusion and mystery were a societal standard.

"Abyss, we have studied the dome and I have the location. We know how the power source is activated and we will power it on again. I offer you a part in it. As we are aware, the dome was built by the ancient Atlanteans and is a source of vital artificial intelligence. A source that can transform our reality and protect against pollution of collective energies. Imagine the potential! We can control our reality. We can control Atlantis." Devon expresses himself with full authority.

Cold silence enters the space as Abyss's energies halt.

This control could lead to a harmonious agreement between the people of Atlantis, or it could bring revolt and power-hungry feuds to the surface. She trembles inside.

"Devon, the dome—you should not touch it. It is far beyond us and holds too great a power. You do not possess the wisdom to activate the dome. We need to meet with the chamber and have a discussion with all parties involved. This dome is way too dangerous for us It was too dangerous for the ancients."

They both understood that the dome was designed to be ruled by none other than the ancients.

"Abyss, we both know that debating this with the chamber will achieve nothing." Devon plays the political card, grasping that if Abyss aspires to be part of the operation, taking it to the chamber would lead to conflicts and arguments." Devon smiled and turned away, understanding that he just put Abyss in a seriously tight space.

"I represent your alliance. I'm going to activate the dome. It's just a matter of time. The power of the dome can heal many Atlantean problems, and we can purify this empire."

"Devon, we must get a Capitol mandate. We don't understand the ancient technology, even ancient struggles; shut it down. "The onerous duty as the AI was too dominant."

Abyss reiterates the riskiness of the task.

She needs time, understanding the fate of Atlantis, perhaps even the human race, can be up to her actions now.

"Where will you use the dome?" Abyss asked in awe.

"It is my intention to explore possible outcomes. You know not all ancients left Atlantis. Our scanners found them in between the dimensions, where time moves remarkably slower. One of our sunsets is a thousand for them—as in stasis, or hibernation. The dome shows its intelligence in many forms. We are still calculating outcomes. I will return tomorrow for my answer," Devon said as he disappeared into a thick blue mist.

Abyss has an extraordinary dispute in her heart. Commitment, however temporary, must be handed over completely.

She can join the exploration, gather information, and pledge her union once the time arises. Curiosity arouses her being, and vibrations unknown and forbidden tempt her more.

"Our understanding of ancient technology is limited to the information allowed to filter down: knowledge filled with warnings, mysteries, stories, and sacred writings. We know ancients disappeared after a widespread infection. We have some understanding of the internal struggle within the colony. We believe that a significant portion ascended through portals within the pyramids and never returned. We assume the remaining beings experienced major collective trauma, as the shared souls abandoned mutual space.

Abyss mixed in her inner guidance, looking for a spark of light to illuminate the road ahead. She pushes deeper in her higher self, her life calling to preserve the current priestess culture and way of life.

Savor the mysteries of the magic of Atlantis, view the knowledge of the ancients, carefully from a distance.

Abyss speaks aloud when opening her eyes. Her head is bowed towards the floor; there is peace in the room; her body language tells it all; she cannot interpret the possibilities just explored. She only feels the challenge will be extensive.

She places her hand on the door.-

"Nothing will be the same." She hears a voice echoing inside and drops a tear onto the marble floor.

CHAPTER 11

Snow-Halo reaches the surface of the water and gasps for air. In the salty water his vision is a rainbow blur. He looks down at the girl, her blond hair tangled around him. With one hand he massages his eyes, while the other feels the beat of her heart. Weak and tender. Swiftly moving, towing her, under a shadow. Sunsets between giant pillars, fingers grasping the grass in the green ground. Carrying her in the brightness, an absurd rate of speed.

"Have no fear; the heart beats. There is something inside you keeping you alive. Dear creature of life, I ask you to wake up from your voyage." Snow-Halo places his hand on her heart, adding pressure. Her heart recognizes strength, the touch of another human. Her beat is stable as he opens his channels. His energy vortexes emerge from dimensions above and her energy follows the spark. They carry life from above in the realms of the gods. The atmosphere in the temple is electrified by the pillars conducting a magnetic carousel of the spectrum of light. Snow-Halo leans over towards her mouth, blowing fresh air into her lungs.

He raises his head. His eyes sparkle with colored light as he holds his hand firm atop her chest. He begins transferring light and energy into her heart. His hand on her heart glows like a purple star. The energy travels from the core into every cell. Vibrating, resonating and shining like a new star. The cosmic breath.

As the gates to the temple close, stillness enters their space. Her heart beats vigorously now. There are sensations all over his body, a pleasurable result of the task accomplished. The evening has turned into night as the stars light up the sky. Snow-Halo embraces her head, caressing her long, wet hair. When her eyes open, he is staring into an emerald soul.

Her eyes are observing her surroundings, seemingly aware of what has just happened.

"I'm feeling safe and revived. I don't remember anything after the underground temple. My desire for answers and communication. His eyes are awakening something familiar to me."

Mirabella allows a broad smile to emerge over her face, gently connecting to Snow-Halo's eyes. He smiles back, enabling her to penetrate deep into his soul, his heart welcoming the penetration. The synchronicity of the heartbeats, the harmony of the breaths.

After the experience, Mirabella has heightened her spiritual sensitivity. At this moment, Snow-Halo is a palette of bright colors and she is the artist to interpret them. A star map and Earth puzzle together. She remembers him; she knows him. Snow-Halo is allowing her to touch the deepest parts of his soul.

Illustrated on the canvas of creation, Mirabella pulls in the pain occurring in both of them. A nucleus of the former star inside them. Damage and collapse of faith in life took place at the junction in the helix of lifetimes. Crossing the river of tears in the temple of darkness. Together in the separation of the blood. She holds the torment, devoted to healing the off-beat of the hearts. Emotions manifest in the temple of pain, overwhelming them, while Snow-Halo and Mirabella gaze at each other, watching the flow of salty tears run towards their lips. Tasting the salty resolution emerge from the pain, reunion, and search of lifetimes. The hands hold stronger as the beat of the heart deepens. It's the only universe they have: reality fades away, their surroundings dim, the temple is gone and the lake recedes. They are alone in their moment.

She pulls herself closer, arching backward while opening the strum of her heart. She climbs slowly into his lap, moving her fingernails towards his spine, sinking them deep into his skin. Electric animation of hallucination in her gaze, as her fingers run up his neck and meet the tenderness of his hair. Snow-Halo pulls her hips into his. She gently bends her head while escorting his lips to her neck. A light touch of the lips in the softness of the skin, the pulse of life the drum of the heart, the taste of salted teardrops trickling down her skin. The emotions of the past/future/now.

The tenseness of the breath as a smile appears. Cruel Passion dancing with the softness of the tenderness.

The uncontrollable desire of mammalian hunger to annex domains lusts.

Ongoing, eternal romance shared by the souls felt within the trembling atoms vibrating indestructible love.

Preparation for the first-kiss descent into the moment.

The Search, taste, feel, touch, and confession, the taste of lips, the sweetness marinated by the salty tears' conjunctions of personal thunder, a string of passion blessed by love gathered an eternity ago.

Snow-Halo and Mirabella wake up to a new sunrise. With them, everything is restored and rotated. The cycle of cosmic maneuvering has altered the focused intent. Lying side by side, studying each other, as the memories return of the love seeded a long time ago. Flowering in the flash of creation, while the bodies gently touch, fingertips travel in the circus of sensations. Smiles and sparkles in the eyes beam out toward the future. They contemplate this magical reconnection in their unique voyage.

"I'm Mirabella, priestess. What's your name?" Mirabella asks gently.

"Snow-Halo, magician," Snow-Halo replies as he gazes into her deep eyes.

"You remember now, as I do?" he asks and tightens the grip on her hand.

"Yes, I do remember our first life together in the future and why we traveled into Atlantis?" she asks, smiling sincerely.

"Exactly. Something we buried deep in our hearts," Snow-Halo replies.

"Perhaps first we eat fruits from the tree and then talk!" Mirabella laughs and runs towards the lake.

"Fruits, hmm sure." Snow-Halo is left behind, viewing the surrounding trees.

CHAPTER 12

Mirabella takes gentle steps towards the lake shore; her bare feet gently massage the round stones. Her movement is graceful. She bends over the mirrored reflection in the lake, watching her image, smiling to herself. Her fingertips eloquently penetrate the crisp surface. She captures water in her hands and sprinkles it onto her face, repeating it multiple times. Once feeling safe and reunited with the lake that Mirabella had nearly died in the day before, she drops her silk wrap and dives. After gently playing with the water, she is afloat, meditating on the turn of events that transpired.

"I see the pattern. I feel this is the moment for something substantial to manifest."

For a majority of Atlanteans, this experience would be sufficient for a life story. Mirabella felt differently.

"This inbound power is something I've not considered or viewed in my meditations before. Will we able to overcome it?" Mirabella leaves the question in the ether. Opening her bright green eyes, breathing deeply, she gazes at the Sun and smiles.

Snow-Halo looking into the temple, observing the light dancing in the recently appeared crystals in the pillars, an original attribute of the sanctuary. Now revealed after the energy work he and Mirabella completed.

He savors each moment, every step he takes, and every emotion inside his heart. The contact between his bare feet and the rocks below him connects to an incredible space within the inside of his mythical reality. Absoluteness of existence, given the enchanting view in front of his eyes, the reflection of the lake overshadowed only by the flowing beauty of Mirabella. He stops and blesses the moment before taking the last steps to the shore.

"I'll be there in a moment!" Mirabella bends her back and dives, reorienting herself under the water and catapulting herself towards the beach. "She is an excellent swimmer. Perhaps she should have been a mermaid." Snow-Halo makes a mental note as he views her approaching. He chooses to sit down on an extensive rock shelf, placing his legs into the water and the self-made tree-branch basket next to him. He bites a piece of fruit, allowing nectar to splash onto his face. A moment later, Mirabella's hands appear next to him.

She extends her hand and grabs a fruit while using the other hand to touch Snow-Halo's neck and offers him a deep kiss.

"I thought we lost each other forever in the year 3,501. Now we meet 35,000 years before it happened, and you want to give me a magician's interpretation of the mysteries and magic of love? Or we can deepen our love on this beach." Mirabella smiles widely and smacks Snow-Halo on his leg. Snow-Halo places his hand on top of hers and smiles with sparkles in his eyes. "Indeed, I remember the recurring nightmare from the year 3,501, when they took me away from you. It haunts me in my dreams and meditations often; only, now I'm able to see more of the trauma." Snow-Halo stops for a moment and connects with Mirabella's eyes. "You've not changed at all, a portrait of Aphrodite, a goddess of beauty." Snow-Halo gently guides his fingertip to follow her face. "Sculptured by the gods," he thinks.

Mirabella puts her hands around him, pulls her body tighter into his, and allows tears to run down.

"We had a time on Earth, and it ended so gruesomely. The behavior of the future humans towards love. Love and relationships policed by artificial systems, emotions buried under a microchip. We rebelled and paid the price.

"I remember my last day on Earth, in the year 3,501. In the morning I went with my sister to do some shopping, to find a dress to wear to our extended-family dinner. I was extremely excited to meet your family, your friends and colleagues, finally! And yes, my sister was looking forward to meeting your friends. She wished a lieutenant or something similar at the space academy would come her way. We, the less-fortunate family, did not save any credits to get ready for the dinner. I must admit that I was quite nervous to meet your dad.

"We purchased the finest brands our government allowance could buy. I left my sister in her accommodation in Silver City and continued toward our home. I remember it like it was just a moment ago. My dress was white and silver. I placed it on the bed, crossed my arms and jumped in the air." Mirabella sighs and takes a deep breath while cementing her connection to Snow-Halo.

"I was in a not-so-fortunate family in that life. I was so happy about our love, our plans, and the peace I had. That gratefulness was divine. The day before, my mom was so proud of me; of the prospect of me working outside the family jobs. It was just beautiful. Then it happened. I heard a door open and ran toward it, expecting you to be there. Four huge shadows appeared, and I felt pain in my heart . . . Then it was over. I looked down at my body and felt my soul leaving the plane of existence, or so I thought."

Mirabella, feeling her heart pounding like a wild horse in the race of its life, places Snow-Halo's hand on her heart.

It's sorrow beyond the smoke of life
A cruel destiny to carry
Sadness of sharp melancholy
Dance of death

Fate carved by judgment, the word of a false god
Melody of rusty sorrow
Captured starlight in an ocean of time

Screams of an Angel of light
Sandpapered story of a whisperer
Melody of melancholy
Collapsed smoke, the shy romance

A breath of empathy
Dancing in the empty room
Lonely clock, ticking in a forsaken universe
Ticking alone, forever.

Snow-Halo moves his body slightly closer to Mirabella, placing his free hand on her shoulders, and plants a kiss on the corner of her forehead. A moment of silence is created as energies form to thought patterns and understanding. He would like to say or do something that allows these powers to release, but there is nothing other than his memories and visions he can add.

"The lives we had were ended in the year 3,501. It left a crater in my heart. Memories arise of the last day. I had not seen you for weeks, back when we spoke via intercom. I missed your presence immensely. I was in space. The assignment was considered dangerous. Your necklace lay against my heart all the while. I typed a message to you in case I did not return to you. I left it hanging on the intercom. The mission went according to plan and the spaceship was inbound to Earth.

I let my colleagues, friends, and family know and entered the shuttle towards home, to you. On the way, something strange occurred. I opened our front door and saw you on the floor. After the moment of lightning-like impact, all else went dark for me; my next memory is in captivity."

Snow-Halo tries to clear the timeline of the future life, not allowing the emotions to take control; he wants to appear strong, even at the point of collapsing.

"*The reading is, the future experience waits, the memories of the soul employed by God, traveled together here and bring the magic in 3,501?*" Snow-Halo asks, looking deeply into Mirabella's eyes; she is now holding his arm in an embrace.

"I always felt that I came to find something from here. I have a feeling it's very close. I am stronger; yet I feel many difficulties are ahead," Mirabella adds.

"Yes, would you like to join me in the Capitol? The annual gatherings are ongoing and I'm already two days late. We can walk through the forest and find the wisdom. Or," Snow-Halo adds, "maybe you have another plan."

"No plans. The Capitol seems like the next step. We need to stop first. I have no clothes, but I know exactly where to go." Mirabella finds some comfort in the upcoming adventure.

"Yes, it's important to look good,'" Snow-Halo adds, and winks at her. They get up and prepare for the hike.

CHAPTER 13

Snow-Halo and Mirabella stand at a juncture in their cre-ation, occurring in their cosmic clock. Together, in an avenue. Reflected by the melody of their hearts; echoing from the chapter of romance.

The ambiance is recognizable. Familiar memories spin the wheel of time. From the age of Aphrodite to an era of alcohol. Romance built with bourbon on the kitchen table. From the luminous luster created by the melody of an angelic choir to the hazy electric guitar on a radio station, the end always the same: drunken by love. Bookmarked is the experience behind the wheel of the ages. They tie their palms together with crossed fingers, holding them tightly while seeking the spark of each other's eyes. Standing tall, facing the descending Sun, catching a broad view of the ground ahead.

Their passage wanders across the muddy waters, escalating toward the mountains and descending beyond the dark forest.

The melody of madness in the beating heart, dancing in the

curiosity of the affectionate moment. The tender smile forming in the expectation of a tender kiss.

> Wishes to stop time, retire from reality.
> Reclaim the domain of soul. Hold her in his arms, allow her softness to waterfall, the fossilized amber of love.
> Drop by drop until an ocean of affection overwhelms the desire residing in the string of a guitar, the brush of a painter, heart of a man.
> Hold onto the moment, pretend you are a feather of an angel, lost in the spiral of time, reaching out to the first sense of destiny.
> The Railway of fate.

Snow-Halo and Mirabella allow the moment to pass, embracing it. A long voyage looms ahead to the capital city of Atlantis. Crossing the forest offers time to explore the energies of each moment of possible adventure. Wilderness sounds echo in the shadows, and sparks of hidden dimensions penetrate reality. Behind them are the moments shared in the temple. Guided by the wisdom gathered from lifetimes, they are reminded of the trauma caused by the continuance of existence. The temple fades in the background, dominated by the forest. Shadows of the trees block the light of the Sun.

Embracing the attraction of mystery, the two enjoy the flavor of adventure's tempting danger. Their harmonious steps drift them forward. Lost in the darkness of the voyage, they are illuminated only by memories of the past, travels to the future, and fantasies of the present. Mirabella and Snow-Halo cover the first few long miles, and silence marks the start of the journey.

Only the wilderness speaks as the birds sing, butterflies fly, and smiles exchange in the shade.

The passage grows deeper into the forest as night's shadows rise and it is time for the moon. Silver shadow of secrets buried in the fabric of time is open. Portal into the subconscious records of all the answers, presented in this gravity.

"Let's camp for a night before we enter the waters and mountains. The area is easier to cross during daytime, as the Sun guides us from the thick forest ray by ray. I feel we have still a lot to discuss, so let us do it in front of a fire." Snow-Halo gives the idea to Mirabella in a soft but confident voice, knowing how tricky the forest can be, with all of the extradimensional creatures in it.

"I have no objection. I'll make the bed. You get the fire," she adds, knowing the next hours will provide answers they are both waiting to receive. Ideas of what will happen in the future, why they are going to Atlantis, and what will happen when they arrive.

CHAPTER 14

Two days ago . . .

She stands at the main palace in the capital city of Atlantis. A serene young lady with chocolate-colored eyes is standing, focused. She is the primary guardian and head of security for the Queen of Atlantis, Anna (aka White Queen), the absolute authority of the capital and allied city states, covering around 75 percent of the land mass of Atlantis but only 30 percent of the spiritual energy available in the collective consciousness.

Some highly evolved temples and individual city states have left the central governing body, preferring to let individual uniqueness and creativity be the rules of life. By communicating, sharing, and respecting other ways of life, it has created two passages for human evolution in the energies of Atlantis. The sovereign city states continue to mature, achieving patience by spiritual practices such as meditation, breathing, Sun gazing, crystal magic, astral travel, etc.

In the capital, collective consciousness has opted for a close relationship with the applied science of crystal computing and nanotechnology. Allowing the population to reach expanded levels of human capabilities, with enhanced psychic and super-human powers and longer life cycles. In the untrained mind/body/spirit complex, this was seen as very dangerous by the independent city states and temples—which often pointed out that the renegade group, the *Black Pyramid,* would not exist if this practice had never taken root.

She, the head of security and right arm of Queen Anna, is the fifth generation of enhanced-nanocrystal humans. She stands at the oval doorway in the entrance of the palace.

She is looming in the shadow of a giant black marble arch, opening up to the skies and leading into the central hallway. This is the private house of the Queen, attached to the main temple of the capital. It's located in midtown on high ground as the rest of the city spirals toward the outskirts. Her golden-brown skin is accompanied by her faint golden aura. Around her, a resonance is created by the nanocrystals in her cells.

She keeps her brown, curly hair cut short and her black, simple uniform holds the small golden symbol of the Royal Guard on her chest. In her belt she carries a portfolio of technology—allowed to use it for defense in tactical situations if manifested.

Her nanocrystals connect in the collective crystal of the temple, facilitating streamlined updates to aggregate points of interest in the capital. Information sharing is instant. All she needs do is to think of what she needs. She is able to see in the darkness, view the additional dimensions, and possess highly evolved psychic abilities and enhanced physical capabilities.

This heightened human competence is also achieved in the independent city states and particularly in the temples. The natural-process master takes decades to equal her nanocrystals. Onyx is much younger than the priest/priestess class in the higher temples and equally skillful.

Onyx feels a gentle electrical buzz in her spine—immediately knowing that the Queen is arriving, as the crystal collective has recorded Anna's energy signature upon her entering the temple's domain. Onyx sees a vision of an interdimensional portal opening inside the Queen's chamber. Understanding that Queen Anna is en route, she prepares her presence.

She drops her gaze from the large arch connecting the temple and the Queen's palace. As she places her hand on the door, the nanocrystals send an encrypted key to unlock it. Onyx sends two messages: one of her own arrival to the Queen, and a message of the Queen's arrival to her colleagues. Onyx arrives at an open space constructed with excellent accuracy. It is built from the finest materials, with pillars and mirror-like material reflecting the stunning views across space. Not as significant as one would believe a woman of her status would have, yet still impressive. The abstract, mirror-like walls create a soothing, nearly amnestic experience as the quicksilver-like material abstractly reflects energies across the room. The dance of shimmering silver light is followed by a beautiful, full-figured woman in a white dress decorated with a selection of the rarest and most valuable crystals of ancient times. Her eyes are pure silver and her white hair is highlighted in silvery tones. The Queen has stepped out of the wall. No one, including Onyx, knows how the wall works or where Queen Anna goes when she disappears inside. Onyx has observed her absence inside the wall for many weeks, yet she does not know where she goes. No one dares to ask, either, as the Queen has kept it a secret for many years.

"Onyx, have you prepared my request?" She voices her question.

"Yes, my Queen, it's waiting for you in the Violet Room," Onyx replies. "Inform all that our meeting starts when the Sun is at its highest point. I will be with you shortly," the Queen commands and walks into the Violet Room.

She takes a few breaths and looks around. She sometimes rests in this room, as it's incredibly magnetic, possessing a field in which she can regenerate and regain re-creation energies in her body. In the middle is a small, purple triangular object. She walks to it and picks it up, along with the dark blue velvet bag next to it. She opens it and approves the contents by nodding her head, smiling widely. Swiftly clicking the top of the triangle open, she places the powder inside the bag into the object and activates it. A soft, mechanical hymn is released as the object has reached optimal resonance. She puts it in her pocket and steps out of the room.

"My Onyx, how do I look?" she asks, looking her deeply in the eye while walking toward her.

"Divine, my Queen," Onyx replies in a gentle, intimidated manner that yet holds a sparkle in her eyes. Queen Anna's strong presence expands around her as she focuses on Onyx and places her hands on her head, pulling her lips to her own and giving her a long kiss.

"We'll continue later," she whispers to Onyx, releasing her grip.

"Yes, my Queen," Onyx replies. She is unsure about the feelings she or the Queen has. Her presence dominates Onyx in such a way that the lines between "Head of Security" and lover blur and she doesn't know whether her emotions are real or programmed.

"Onyx, it's the first time in a century that the heads of political and spiritual communities are present in the same assemblage. We will work and create together in the coming days to regain the peace and order of our continent before it's too late," Anna informs Onyx while keeping her hypnotic gaze locked onto her.

"Yes, my Queen. Security has been expanded and our ships are patrolling the nearby skies and dimensions. Nearly all participants have arrived, with just a few en route. Military forces are grounded, standing by for the arrival of the commander's cruiser, which was last sighted in the mountains," Onyx reports, scanning updates from the crystal computer.

"Exceptional, Onyx. Request an escort. I am ready. Also, send two of my ships to keep an eye on our dear commander. I would like to know what he is up to." Anna steps closer to Onyx and places her palm on her face. She looks deeply into her eyes, whispering, "You have always been special and you know it. A bright future awaits you."

"Thank you," Onyx responds, feeling strong sensations run through her body.

CHAPTER 15

The conference starts as the Queen walks into the room, her escort alongside her, stopping at the door, while the Queen makes her way to the throne in front of her audience. As she steps in front of her seat, she scans the room and focuses on the few empty slots. Still standing, she places her hand on the nearby scanner. Her identity confirmed, the conference begins.

"Members of the council, I welcome you on this cosmic day—a day to be remembered across Atlantis. We are gathered here with a need to shift our continent's consciousness. For the past few months we have studied the super-crystals that reflect our future's timeline. All of you are aware and have taken part in the descent of our continent. Here, today, we stand as a group. We stand as a legion tasked with guiding our people toward the next start. The next seed of life. We are separated from the outskirts of creation by the boundaries of our imagination. We implement instruments of belief and supervision, but how can we expect to move forward if our towns are walled by systems of understanding?"

As the Queen concludes her opening remarks, she looks around the table and out at the crowd. She sits in her seat and rests her arms on the table, noticing the transparent ceiling above and observing the Sun at its highest point.

"Thank you, Queen Anna. All present would like to address the growing concern about the imbalance on our continent between current political and spiritual arrangements agreed on after the last war. Unions and leaders were overturned and here we face the same fate. The Capitol has forced its outlying cities and temples to find safety within each other due to the lack of military force present anywhere but the capital itself. The Capitol's technological advances do not resonate with the free temples. They are only humans, with no technological forces as we have here. We must protect them." The secretary of the free temples pauses for a moment and observes the tiniest of reactions surfacing amongst his colleagues.

"Also, if I may, we live in constant terror of the Black Temple society, which grows stronger each day. By our continental agreement, 90 percent of the forty council seats must agree on use of military force, which is why our defense forces haven't been touched since the war!" He sighs, feeling the sadness rising from his heart. Holding back tears, he breathes deeply to release his anger.

"Due to the rusting of our forces, our communities across the continent have devised their own weapons systems. The Capitol boasts only twenty small destroyers. This is not capable of defending us from attacks from outer spaces and dimensions! Are we in touch with any allies? No! Who is the enemy of our destroyers? No one but us!" Max looks into the eyes of the

Queen—his inner being trembling, as he understands the challenge he has presented to his highness. Might she be inclined to action instead of a purely ceremonial role? He feels the power at her disposal, and his experience heightens with frustration.

"Secretary Max, our fleet consisting of twenty destroyers gives us some protection from the *Black Pyramid* and rebel domains of the Capitol as well other distant parts of Atlantis, like your island. As you're certainly aware, the Royal Guard possesses a modest fleet of air and space units if you so need."

Anna's hypnotic glare penetrates Max's soul, directly entering his deepest aspects of being. She's able to communicate using her energies, a skill perfected in the past. Max feels the shift in his energy field and understands the commitment he made by challenging her.

"Queen Anna, the Royal Guard and Capitol are overpowering the free states in every respect. Your military is stationed here and will only act in case of a direct threat from the Black Temple. The Royal Guard is protecting only those with royal blood and those within the Capitol domain. Seven seats stand empty here today. Tell me, Queen, how would we vote for military stations today? Why did enough of us not show up for a quorum to vote?" Max expresses his dissatisfaction with flamboyant hand movements and heightened verbal tones. Now, with not only the scope of the situation exposed but the Queen herself exploited, the energy of his violation hangs like a cloud over the room. His cries are met with silence from Queen Anna. Quietness takes hold in the room and a series of deep breaths are released by the members. Energies tense as the Queen's response is awaited.

A gentle female voice arises: "Hello, I'm Amina, representing the village and temple of Theo on the outskirts of the capital. Mr. Secretary, I resonate deeply with your words, and we admire the island you come from. We respect the leadership of our Queen, especially now that since the war she's rebuilt Atlantis from the ground up. The resources she had were limited at the time and it is still a wonder to us at the progress her highness has made." Amina shifts her attention to Queen Anna and receives a gentle nod from her, signaling her to continue.

"Not too long ago, our temple was surrounded by the forest. Now the capital has expanded into our village. Understanding technological advances that the city has taken and the implants its residents have sustained, our daily interaction with the capital has made our hearts wonder: are we the same species anymore? When you enhance your consciousness, body, and spirit with crystal implants connected to the mainframe, aren't you taking a step toward the fate warned by the ancient texts?" Amina ends her emotionally painted speech and drops back into her seat.

The large, glossy table in front captures the reflection of a sizable man. His shadow seems to cover the room as he stands, gaining the arena's attention.

"Lady of Theo, implants have been extended, outshining the human capabilities known to us for many years. The Capitol created this technology to reach the stars; to liberate the dimensions that, before this, hung just over the horizon. Our human citizens have been enhanced with the ability to travel to the distant cosmos. We welcome forward-thinking people into our community, all of them using our science at their own free will!" The man, currently appointed the Minister of Sciences, stands dominatingly facing the crowd.

Max, feeling that this might be another typical convention that leads nowhere in regard to answers and cooperation, decides to verbalize his feelings. "We talked of the dominance of the Capitol in all aspects, as well as the expected uprising coming toward our free states that will eventually bleed into the capital and across Atlantis. We request an audit of the Capitol's technology. Who has access to it? We need to know. The free states believe there are Black Temple spies in the highest ranks of the Capitol's science team. Otherwise, how do we explain the precisely technological construction of the *Black Pyramid*?" Max can't take it anymore. Young and fiery, he is part of the new wave of leaders manifested across Atlantis. He looks toward Amina, hoping she'll join in his outcry, but is only met with a smirk and a question: "Perhaps someone has found the ancient texts?"

"Everyone! The message was transmitted to you and you came together, except the missing seven, so let us truly find solutions! We all received the signal, we all replied to it, and we all must make these decisions. Rise up in support of the unknown dimensions ready for us to explore. Unite in the love of our people and domains. We are here together to lead this continent into the future. The Brotherhood can work together to locate and end the *Black Pyramid* before it's too late!" Queen Anne gasps for air and nods her head to the leader of the Brotherhood.

"Brother and Sisters, as you've noticed, the seven that did not make it here cannot be part of this process now. We will proceed with our gathering under the guidance of Queen Anna. Afterwards, we will reconnect with our friends and discover the reasons behind their absence. The Order, Black Order, Black Temple, and *Black Pyramid*, you may know, has been tracked by our teams for years. The Brotherhood lost many of our finest scientists and priests to the Black Queen Mary after disputes in council. In many aspects, for a long time, the Order has been technologically more advanced, but now it's also more active. The number of attacks is multiplying. We believe something massive is coming. We do not know who the leading members of this dark-temple society are or their location at any point in time. We can only use energies to track them. Recently, we have measured the quantum spectrum and can safely assume that they relocated yesterday. We can only estimate where they are and follow their movements a few sunsets after they have settled into surrounding power flows. We are here to find solutions and ensure cooperation among all cities and temples to stop them before they take next step." Alder, the leader of the Brotherhood, nods to his peers and returns his attention to the beautiful White Queen.

Queen Anna stands up and reaches into her pocket, placing a pyramid on the table. "We will have a creative moment now." As soon as she puts the object on the table, a flash of light appears from within. The meeting is transferred into the mainframe like a substance flowing through the body. "We will regroup in the space below us. There are conference rooms for each group. Names and positions are assigned on each door. Let's get to work." She smiles and exits the room as her escort returns to her side.

CHAPTER 16

Back in the mountains, Abyss is troubled by the decision she has to make. As a high priestess, she has enormous influence over the independent city states, the balancing power to the Capitol.

Her heart was wishing for a crystal-clear guidance, transparent as a glass of still water; at least, Abyss hoped.

Abyss was left in a consciousness limbo, not sure of either of the timelines she surveyed in her powerful meditation.

She powers up and summons Devon to return.

Devon promptly marches into her chamber and rests his eyes on hers.

Standing tall and strong, he waits in silence.

"Devon, I'm transparent to you. We don't understand the technology of the ancients, not even the spiritual practices they had.

The dome is hiding a secret—one that's beyond the knowledge of the priesthood." Abyss breathes in, firms up, and steps close to him.

"We have done everything, translated the language, studied the crystal designs, and experimented with the technology." Abyss hesitates and disconnects from the chat.

Mr. Prime Selected Devon holds his silence and waits for her to return.

"Devon, I'm joining the voyage; the result of the exhibition hopefully will turn positive under my supervision!" Abyss heatedly blurts out, then clearly informs Mr. Prime Selected, "All eyes are on you!"

She holds time a hostage while reverberating her divine energies and penetrates Devon's being. Making her essence felt, not just heard.

"Agreed. I accept. Collectively we operate. I'll signal the cruiser to transport you; prepare your crew to board at midday." Devon communicates his plans.

"Agreed. We will be ready," she concluded and slowly turned her back and walked away.

Devon stepped onto the temple platform and observed the incredible scenery colored by the passing fogs shading the rays of the sun.

He allows a few minutes to pass and breathes in before signaling to the base.

"Base commander, execute the following order: launch a heavy warship over the borders of the Temple of Abyss. Light load of marines and officers." Devon stops and waits for the commander.

The line rattles slightly before the commander replies.

"Base copy and registered. Cruiser *Neptune*, at your disposal. Arrival in the afternoon."

At this very time, Devon receives a new request from cruiser *Senjo*, now located somewhere in the mountain range.

"Mr. Prime Selected, its commander, at the bridge of *Senjo* on standby for your arrival. We discovered the power source of the dome and chamber," Commander Alfa notified Devon, unable to hide the excitement in his statement.

"Chamber? Refresh me, Commander," Devon demanded,

"A hallway leading to a massive chamber. We're working on the route to enter by. The entrance is composed of a material we don't recognize. The progress is moderate for now, and scans confirm the inside contains a massive metallic object and viable life forms.

"Remain there until our arrival. Anything more, Commander?" Devon adds in a determined tone.

"Yes, the communication systems are functioning at the limit. Radiation from the power source is creating a disturbance around our network. We're sending a probe to relay messages and to scan. Examination of the information displays two Capitol destroyers in this region; they are a distance away but aware of our presence." The commander informed Devon of the situation, with slight concern in his voice.

"Commander, keep your eyes on the Capitol destroyers. Any movement, report immediately," Devon added, while vigorously assessing the new information.

This wasn't good news to Devon. Capitol can't follow the project at this point.

"Capitol should be in lockdown and concentrated on the gathering. What are the royal destroyers doing so far away?" Devon thinks and runs through alternative options to lure them away from the dome.

"It will quickly escalate, once they see another cruiser approach the mountains. In response, Capitol will dispatch one pair of destroyers, the hierarchy will involve themselves, etc." He viewed the outcomes and decisions the Capitol guard would make.

"I plan a diversion to lure them away." Devon is sure; he can't allow the plan to be revealed. Devon produces a quick idea, something to provide added leverage, and contacts the base.

"Base, send cruiser *Minotaur* into the dark forest; captain it in an automatic sweep of the area."

Devon informed the military base, with determination: "*Minotaur* now close to the capital; the trauma will spread, and the Royal Guard will concentrate its actions on *Minotaur* rather than *Neptune* and *Senjo*. *Neptune* will take the long route and conceivably stay in stealth." He gives a heads-up and expresses confidence in the plan.

Sometime a little later the words "We're ready to go" echo in Devon's ears. Abyss moves lightly towards him, accompanied by her twelve temple guards. She has taken off the gentle, breathing dress and geared up for the adventure in a tight, black modern dress, sculping a picture of her beautiful body.

"After you, Lady. Cruiser *Neptune* is idling inside the temple territorial borders. Permission to allow it in?" Devon is earnestly watching Abyss for a reaction to the question. The temples are no-go areas for any military and Capitol ships, and granting permission to Devon's cruiser would make it the first ship to enter after the war.

"No, our shuttle will transport us; no teleportation today, Mr. Prime Selected," Abyss informs them, while a silver tear-shaped shuttle lands on the temple deck.

In a few moments, the dark gray battleship *Neptune* appears from the clouds. Abyss steps forward to have a good look at it.

At about a half kilometer long and two hundred meters tall, it's an impressive sight. It's for the long haul, shaped in a thin, oval, with four large engines attached to the back of the ship; he, pauses at each engine.

"It does look beautiful," one of the temple guards thinks out loud.

While Abyss turns towards Devon, "You ever take her into space?"

"No, we cannot. As you know, primary batteries and hyperdrive would need an authorization code from the central crystal," Devon adds and smiles forcefully back to Adele.

"I feel she is powerful, the *Neptune*; looking at her energies I sense her fate is secure." Adele gasps for air and gazes at the *Neptune*, while the shuttle enters into the belly of the *Neptune*.

CHAPTER 17

Mirabella and Snow-Halo are about to arrive at the edge of the dark forest. The setting of the sun and the rise of a dark fog foreshadows the impending riddle, the dilemma of a mystery lying just ahead at the capital. A sudden frostiness is traveling across Mirabella's silky skin, shivering down her spine. Her breath constructs icy clouds as they gently move ahead.

Snow-Halo's fingertips catch the bitter frost from descending ice crystals, his feet rooting in the gentle vegetation on the forest floor. The hail of coldness emerges and jolts through his veins. He feels a sudden drain of his magic. The pair stops for the moment, connecting through mutual memory. Their eyes like speculums into the gateway of the spirit. In stillness, the highest communication occurs while the heartbeats are synchronized. Snow-Halo pulls Mirabella closer to him, her lips pressing on his, spilling the emotion of their timeless caress in the wicked hailstorm. They are wrapped in the cycling, blinding, eternal kiss of the spirit: the experience of a binding sensory view into one's soul.

"The capital home is close by," Snow-Halo whispers to Mirabella, who replies with a nakedly tender smile. Their steps, in tandem, carry a warm promise, circling around them like the arms of their very essence. All around them, ice crystals gently flow toward the ground, painting the scenery pure white. Mirabella extends and opens her hand, allowing snowflakes to travel to her glowing palm. Her flaming, rosy lips touch the cold drops of water. Her eyes move to meet Snow-Halo's in the absorption of this bright, blind moment. Snow-Halo is observing an ambrosial sensation entering into his spirit. The spark in her eyes revealing a flare in his heart, dancing in a flow of amity, allowing a flash to burst.

They open the door and enter as an array of crystals light up, illuminating the space in a dark violet hue. The flames of the fire before them dance like moving paintings of the shadows on the walls. Snow is tenderly descending from the heavens, sheltering the sphere.

His fingertip travels down her long strands of hair, her spine curving in an arch, extending her neck for a kiss. They escape from their loneliness and enter into the Elysium of unity; the triangle of immortality. Their lips find the fire as their bodies wrap around each other, tearing each other apart as the fire's painted shadows flicker. Confessions of lust become a dance of fantasies. A laugh of destiny in the blindness of empyrean love. Hips in a fever of the fieriness, melody ancient in a steady beat of life, the ecstasy of lifeblood. In the moment of entities, she shines the silver light her eyes transmit, the golden light a beam of wisdom, her body embraced by the spark of love. Sparks and then darkness.

A hymn-like note wakes Snow-Halo to a new reality. Mirabella walks naked toward the window. As the fire casts glowing paintings on her body, she looks out and hums a gentle melody. Snow-Halo follows her dance and smiles. Feeling his eyes locked onto her body, she turns around and smiles.

"Beautiful. It's snowing in the valley. Something new must come," she says to Snow-Halo as she walks toward him. "Nice place you have here. Why don't you stay here more often?"

"Still snowing?" Snow-Halo asks as he pulls Mirabella's body closer to his. She willingly finds a relaxed position and offers her body to his caress. "I visit here when a path brings me to the capital. I've always loved this nest; it just happened I had to go searching for a deeper connection." Snow-Halo explains his reasoning while holding a caring gaze into her eyes. "I see. So how come you did not go for the temples?" Mirabella asks. "I left them behind a long time ago," he replies and withdraws his connection from her by tilting his head toward the ceiling. Mirabella can feel the presence of a dark emotion in his heart and places her hand above it, reaching deeper than his skin. Her love penetrates the darkness buried deep in his heart. "Shall we continue toward the center temple?" Snow-Halo asks, wanting her to leave healing for another time. "Yes, my dear!" she adds and jumps on top of him.

CHAPTER 18

Snow-Halo and Mirabella immersed in the abyss of the bottomless, borderless dream of the eternal spirit. Where the essence exists in a timeless spiral, circle in eternity.

Beginning in the saintly space of consciousness, the interpretation of a dream.

Snow-Halo enters into a hall of an ancient temple, a cradle of his creation. The fog supplements a layer of mysticism, satisfying the illuminating fire in the background.

The gentle vibration of a melody echoes in the corridor; the dance of notes escorts him into the hidden memories. His steps are gently grinding to a halt, seemingly a black crystal wasteland, an endless and everlasting road towards the unknown.

Mirabella, breathing in a dome of brightness, blinded by the blazing light, surrounded by the aurora of illumination, circles the vault, her feet touching in hot white sand. Her white dress glazed like a star.

She dances on the rhythm of tranquility and embodies the ambiance of light.

> The sinking steps, drowning on the ageless anxiety of
> lost souls
> The illusion of the false identity in reality
> The shimmer of conscious realization of the fallacy
> The hope of a shelter in the darkness of the night
> The darkest hour of our lives
> The falsified belief of the temple of the heart and
> denial of reality
> A sweet sword of destiny, reaching out to you
> The mirror reflection on the river
> in the return of the lovers in a union of fate
> Pure dream on a beautiful morning

Snow-Halo strays forward—his trail masked by isolation, created misfortune. His limbs sinking deep on the dark sand of solitude, the heaviness of the voyage.

Mirabella is floating on the bubble of illumination, dancing on her featherlike emotions of imagination.

Directly and instantly, she is watching Snow-Halo, her eyes behind the illumination.

Steadily Mirabella shortens the distance between them and captures a thought from her heart.

Gradually Snow-Halo welcomes Mirabella in his presence in the dark path he railed in.

The luster of the vibrant light surrounds Mirabella as she spins in a spiral in the landscape covered by a mysterious fog, illuminating their destiny.

Opening a bond, mediating the choice. Snow-Halo decides either to stay in the reality of now or sculpt a new presence.

Mirabella extends her hand, reaching Snow-Halo; he grips her hand vigorously. The bright droplet surrounding Mirabella thrills as the fog fades away; discharge emerges, and Sky opens, allowing Sunbeams to enter in.

An absoluteness of infinite fullness holding the touch; flowers would grow to place the kiss water might rain; closing the eyes, could feel the feelings, a heartbeat of a thousand suns. A new reality is born.

Morning, and Snow-Halo and Mirabella wake up from the old reality in the house they slept in last night. Mirabella opens her eyes together with Snow-Halo, and they look at each other; she extends her hand and brushes his face. Gives him a smile and kiss. "Let's get you shaved and go for the gathering. You need to be immensely strong today!" she adds and leaves the bed, leaving Snow-Halo for the moment.

CHAPTER 19

The weather reverts to a gentle bath of raindrops. Snow-Halo and Mirabella breathe in the crisp air, smile, and savor a conscious picture of every moment they had in the shelter. Securely they start raising the ridge upwards; the natural and elegant granite building stone leads from the outer circle into the center of the capital. The outer zone, where the villa is located, is a house for the soul who wants to materialize in peace and harmony. Nature, the full boundary between mysteries of the dark forest, a shield from the expanding capital and the technological misuse.

The circular tracks of the Capitol compress towards the center; each layer strives to further compress living and reality. The buildings rise high in the sky; movement and chaos tenses as the population is forced to squeeze into a puny space. In the middle is the temple, the palace of the white queen and her royal government. A large real estate only for her administration and the Royal Guard.

"Something weird is going on besides the gathering; I feel it—strange restlessness in my energies." Mirabella speaks to Snow-Halo and points out two Capitol destroyers speeding towards the dark forest.

"Yes, rarely do we see ships outside of the capital on a gathering. Something must be happening." Snow-Halo validates her thinking.

"We are on the edge of a split, and I sense multiple timelines. We worked intensely to balance the broken energies of Atlantis; it's difficult when the Capitol has such a massive influence over the population.

Mirabella shares her concerns and rather dark perspective on the Capitol and Atlantis.

"True, several powers are in transit! And these powers will continue to move ahead. I observed an obscure *Black Pyramid* ship in the same forest the destroyers went into." Snow-Halo discusses the situation and shares his concern about powers showcasing their capabilities.

"Agreed. The Queen, who is pathologically up her ass about security, is sending in heavy guns. Something is going on, trust me!"

Mirabella cements her suspicion and stares Snow-Halo in his eyes.

For a brief moment they smile, appreciating the connection and experience of sharing. Nevertheless, the critical thoughts of recent events arise, and Snow-Halo and Mirabella continue to speculate.

After a long walk, Mirabella and Snow-Halo arrive at the inner circle of the city, a last ring before the Capitol temple.

It administers to the elite of Atlantis, including all the firms operating in the palace: the Royal Guard, the government, the servants, and entertainment. Lately it largely focuses on propaganda about the superiority of the Capitol and slanders the temple souls and their backward belief systems.

A large, towering multimetal fence separates the palace from the inner circle; its design is aesthetic and functional. Tilting at an angle, this copper-colored fortification sports a beautiful waterfall, circling left to right. Reflecting the natural light, being a forthright beam of Sun from a clean sky or soft moonlight, spongy dancing from the night sky.

"You think they're here to keep people outside or the government inside?" Snow-Halo teases Mirabella.

And she doesn't hesitate to answer, "Keep them inside to work and work! More taxes and more laws!" And she laughs at them.

"Mirabella, shall we?" Snow-Halo aims for the main gate and waits for Mirabella's approval to enter in.

"Wait a moment. A past master I had has a residence a street from here. Can we visit her quickly?" Mirabella halts and places her finger on her lips.

"I got a powerful urge to visit her and ask a few questions; after all, she is a Capitol insider and sincere mentor," she continues and turns a charming expression to Snow-Halo.

"Hmm, I take the point. Let's visit her," Snow-Halo replies and gently places his hand to her shoulders.

The following moment, they are hiking in an energetic street, in a community of higher-class Atlanteans dressed in beautiful white and golden clothes, each unique to the person wearing it. A small contrast to Snow-Halo and Mirabella, with their unceremonious violet and turquoise assemblage. To their surprise, they attract several stares from the local population. "I have an impression the Capitol has transformed in past years; the district is acting in a manner I can't recall, judgmental!" Snow-Halo shares his anxiety and receives a concerned nod from Mirabella.

After a significant time spent shuttling among the masses, they arrive at the front of a white marble door illuminated by a golden-lion emblem.

Mirabella smoothly taps on the entrance, while Snow-Halo observes the crowd crisscrossing the beautiful avenue. A little boulevard just behind the first ring established Atlantean decoration, with towering columns, water streams, flowers, and a small market area. "Mirabella, I'm seeing there are no couples, families, or groups; all of the souls are traveling singly." Snow-Halo is baffled by the change in the Atlantean society. "Yes, quite a few years ago, this avenue was full of families and lovers, humans having a playful time. You are right, and I'm afraid of it," she replies in pain.

The door opens slowly, and the face of an older women appears from the dark hallway. "It's me, Mirabella, Auntie. Let us in," Mirabella says. "Auntie?" Snow-Halo queries and sharpens his eyebrows at her. "Mirabella, you came to see me?" The maturer woman blasts a high-pitched welcome, scaring the birds parked next to the door and drawing not-so-welcome additional attention.

"Come in," she adds and opens the entranceway thoroughly; as Mirabella and Snow-Halo move in, they view a, moderately furnished room for one individual, decorated with centuries of memories and moments.

Mirabella and Snow-Halo follow the lady, who is wearing a long white dress; at the back the dress is designed with the symbol of a golden lion. "Your auntie?" Snow-Halo whispers to Mirabella, "Yes, long story. Tell you later," she adds hastily and continues to walk forward; all of them arrive in a round room. A secret area of worship, an extraordinary power resonating on it.

"Mirabella, how are you, my darling, and why have you come back here? You must know it's extremely dangerous?" She questions her with her sharp silver eyes, exposing the pale whiteness of her appearance. Snow-Halo stands still and reminds himself of the stories he read about the order of lionesses when he was studying the silver energies. Silver lion, hiding below the Golden Lion an order of priestess who only celebrates starlight, and only the soft night light. He found them to be unique in the Atlantean realm of magic, a rare group.

CHAPTER 20

Yesterday, Maximillian and Amina perfected a synergy amongst themselves while dually blocking the Queen's requests. They had each expressed profound worries for the state of Atlantis. In turn, this shared viewpoint initiated a well-rooted connection between them.

Now Maximillian and Amina sit in lotus position inside the temple gardens, catching the noon sunrays in the utterly exclusive setting, surrounded by polished, transparent crystal walls and filled with views of the wildest flowers.

Amina is a youthful priestess politician from the small village of Theon. She is filled with euphoria today, as her dedication to her cause has reached a height of faithfulness. "Maximillian, allow me to hold your hands, take a peek into your essence, and feel the palpation of your heartbeat," Amina voices in a deeply relaxed tone, granting her words a dance on Maximillian's heart.

Maximillian rests his eyes softly on Amina's presence, embodying and adoring each spark of the light she beams. Her clothing today reflects her purity: a long, white dress travels like a snake upon her body, while delicately collected tiny crystals sparkle in rivalry with her smile. "Amina, you are free to enter my world and feel the beat of my heart," he admits as he closes his eyes and grips Amina's hands. He's suited today in all-black clothing with a golden circle decorating the backside of his coat. As an inexperienced leader and the son of a dying commander of a prosperous island state, Maximillian is encountering unusual feelings while with Amina. It may be an opportunity to broaden his depth toward worship of a heart.

Maximillian rests in the sunlight for a moment while strong intentions pierce the light and breach both of their hearts. A spinning whirl of memories appears in a pulse of pain. Black ink on an empty paper—a word never scripted down, left to dry without meaning. The beams of light gather on the pillars, forming a storm of golden light, like a cyclone around their lotus figures. Amina's eyes sparkle from the reality above and she reaches out, saying, "The ink is wet. Script your destiny." They hold on, gripping tighter as the cyclone of golden light enters into Maximillian's heart, catapulting him into the soft green grass behind him. His young adult body is in great agony, and it's the moment when his consciousness flickers off.

"Dad, where am I?" he enquires, standing in an astral projection next to his father's deathbed. Maximillian is embodying his discomfort, all the while trying to hold onto his power; the astral experience, well known in the realms of Atlantis, is still new to him. His dad ruled the island and his family with a military mentality, focusing and fortifying the strengths of the people and himself.

Advancing weaknesses that would only create an average outcome was out of the question! When he was younger, Maximillian's senses drew him toward the temples and studies of the energies, but he was never able to entirely leap into the world of magic. His schooling allowed open observation, but limited engagement—it was his father's way.

"Son, my time is about to come. The portal has opened for me, and anti-gravity is pulling me from my body. I don't have much time. When you return home, take my flagship, the frigate *Colonel of the Guard*, and take my body into deep waters behind the ancient ruins on the Blue Island. I carry my secret with me." He turns his head, showing a face where the rivers of wisdom run deep though his skin and blue eyes have turned to silver pearls. His breath, like a breeze on shallow sand, travels silently from his lungs delivering this string of words. "Dad?" Maximillian repeats, allowing his tears to form questions on his face. "Son, I kept an eerie secret from you and the family . . . and from the island." The old admiral repeats this phrase and touches Maximillian's astral projection with his fingers, slightly amused, observing his hand slice through it. "I cannot understand. Dad, what are you speaking of? Is this a dream?" Maximillian questions the reality he's in. "Son, we have the Blue Tablet. During the last civil war, it was discovered by *Colonel of the Guard* and its crew. I was captain."

The admiral takes a deep breath as if he's sure it's his last. A sigh of relief, a witty smirk, and a fountain of melancholy wrapped in one. "Tensions had broken into individual conflicts. Our neighbors had allied with the Emperor as we, a proud military island, had an oath with the Prime Selected." He coughs and places his hand on top of his chest before continuing: "We believed that the Emperor had infected a third-party race, the same life form as those who created the Blue Tablet. Together with the local temple, *Colonel of the Guard's* sensors tracked it to the Blue Island. The dilemma ensued, as we knew that *Colonel of the Guard* was monitored by the Emperor as well as the current Prime Selected. The submersible ship was launched deep down underwater to hide me and my crew. But they're all gone now. Well, soon enough they will be," he adds.

"Dad, I'm confused," Maximillian says.

"The power will be transferred to you, once I'm gone. Go to my ship. My cabin is open for you and you will find a map to the Blue Tablet.

"Be careful. The alien object is powerful," the admiral adds as he observes his son Maximillian's astral body fade. He gives a gentle glance across the royal-purple room decorated with tasteful art: the alluring open view of the sea framed by white silk curtains, the waves hitting on the gargantuan stones and splashing in a burst of white foam. There he is in his purple uniform—stylish and ready to close his eyes forever.

"Maximillian, Max, wake up!" He hears the soft but alarmed voice of Amina slowly and firmly pulling him back to his body. Not knowing if he feels upset or blessed to hear her voice, Maximillian opens his eyes.

"Dad? Amina? What's happening?" he asks.

"Dad?" Amina asks in response.

"You went somewhere? The gathering starts soon. We need to go in."

"No, I need to contact my home," Maximillian demands.

"You know that nearly all communication is forbidden during the gathering. Why, what happened?" she enquires.

"I have a bad feeling. Let's skip the early part, okay? I'll explain on the way," he adds as he holds her hand.

CHAPTER 21

Qali is standing on the bridge of the *Black Pyramid* command center. "A powerful statement, the cabal has created with this technological marvel. It shall soon land on top of the Capitol building and assume its place as the capstone." This thought pleases him. The interstellar ship packs superior firepower that's powerful enough to take down the armed forces and the old cruiser. The Black Queen has also indicated the Capitol will not fire a single shot. The destroyer fleet would have caused a scrap of resistance.

It's his day and today's attire reflects the power he will unleash. He wears a matte black robe with sinister red embellishments. He has taken double injections today, causing his awareness and focus to run at 150 percent. Absolutely nothing can distract him. "Stations: I want full diagnostics for the ship. Confirm all payloads on the delivery missile and run the latest weather report. The clouds need to spread even!" Qali commands the technicians on the bridge and turns toward his tactical team. "Less than twenty-four hours until the strike.

"Have you calculated the optimal route?" he questions while inspecting his troops.

The octagon-shaped command center allows a 360-degree view of the ship and its progress. Qali's throne sits directly in the middle in a metal, sharp-edged chair that echoes authority. Qali steps towards it, sits down, and begins a general overview of the crew: name, rank, and station are called out by each team member. He comprehends that the only deficiency in the Masterplan is his officers and crew. They're surely not battle-hardened leaders such as the those of the Prime Selected. The Capitol even has a unique technology to compensate for laziness and designs powerful enhancement drugs to keep their force running at top speed.

The Capitol will be able to send only a destroyer fleet and palace guard, which will not be sufficient. The population will bow down at the minute of the Queen's capture. Prime Selected and the armed-force cruiser fleet can circle and cause massive damage to the Black Temple society inside the *Black Pyramid*. Our Queen has ordered them to use their firepower as a safeguard for the ships we plan to override. Use of the heavy weapon systems would be possible if 95 percent of consultants agree and critical mass is not present at the gathering. Qali feels that if he goes toe to toe with Capitol destroyers and perhaps a couple of frigates from the islands (their cruisers can't do much against him without prime weapons) he has a slight edge: surprise and firepower! The battle will cease if the strategy and tactics hold up to the Masterplan. The Black Queen's army is made of older, scorned men and women, maintaining their agility and appearance only through nanotechnology. The rest are children stolen from their mothers. They are not soldiers—they're weak, protected by the Dark Queen's magic. Qali has no respect for anyone but himself and the Black Queen, but that doesn't matter. This is personal.

"It's time! Initiate the drive!" Qali commands and rises up from his chair. A sharp, electric hum echoes across the bridge to the *Black Pyramid* as the ion power sources awake; the bridge is covered in piercing red light. Vibrations on the deck are tense as Qali observes the 360-degrees-underwater perspective—a dark view about to be transformed. "Operator, take us above!" he shouts. Above the surface there is a picturesque setting: the serene lake in the middle of the dark forest, a mirror-like surface reflecting the sunrays, the symphony of nature and roaring animals in an absolute harmony. The piercing penetration is accompanied by a blast from the bottom of the lake. A ship of destruction breaks the surface and rises, hovering above the lake 's exterior. The *Black Pyramid,* on the other side of the lake, experiences a disruptive vibration. The bridge guard is now on full alert. Qali and his ship are out in daylight. This is the sign of something terrible. "All crew to their stations! Take us to our first coordinates."

"Sir, we have contact. A *Neptune*-class cruiser on the north side of the forest about 250 kilometers from our location." Qali jumps onto the screen, alarmed and horrified. "*Neptune?* What are they doing here? That fleet should be on the ground. That's why it's easy pickings as our initial target," Qali quickly processes the information.

"Do they see us?" he asks the operator. "Not sure for now. I believe they have not detected us," the operator answers. "They are heading in this direction. They will detect us in a few minutes' time," the operator informs him.

"If we're spotted, *Neptune* will relay our position and blow the Masterplan to shreds! Go around it and improvise, or take the *Neptune* cruiser head-on!" Qali processes his options quickly. "Operator, start the secondary ion drive," he commands. "Yes, sir," the operator replies as he enters the coordinates into the mainframe. The ominous black spacecraft accelerates quickly away, building a distance between it and the cruiser.

CHAPTER 22

Devon and Abyss stand at the face of an immensely wide golden gate. A legion of Prime Selected officers and elite soldiers stand behind them. Further behind them, one of the four *Neptune* cruisers hovers next to the mountaintop. Two Capitol destroyers blink on the cruiser's detection system and they observe them from a distance.

"The lost answers could be there in the *Black Pyramid*. The secrets of the ancients. We could hold the destiny of humanity," Abyss ponders while looking up at the gate.

"The key to the dome and more ancient technologies is down there," Devon assures himself while observing his technician's eager hacking attempts.

"Any progress, Cadet?" He issues the question impatiently.

"Yes, sir. The code is working," the cadet replies.

Abyss circles around and lays her view on the passing white clouds as she ponders the meaning of the weather's seasons.

The tempo of her breath beats to the balance of life within her heart. She asks herself if some treasures should stay hidden and buried in the ground—never to be seen or touched again. The beautiful view from the high mountaintop caresses her eyes and reflects a horizon of angelic design—clouds passing through sunrays, illuminating the green paradise.

"Devon, I feel this is way too big for Atlantis to handle. We're held together by an inch!" She expresses her worries to him with ardent intent.

"Abyss, it's too late. We must report our finding to the Queen." Devon turns around and conveys his opinion.

Abyss knows this is best for now.

"Commander of the *Sao*, sir, there has been an unusual intrusion in this patrol area. May I request further instruction?" the cadet in front of him asks as a clattering transmission enters Devon's crystal directly. Abyss recognizes Devon's disturbed body language. She makes the decision that she will enter into his energy and witness what he's experiencing at this moment. She closes her eyes and enters a deep state of transcendent consciousness. She enters into a cocoon of many dimensions. She passes a million faces and scenes as she focuses her intent on Devon and travels in his direction. She attaches herself to his energy within moments, while he feels only a slight pinch. With her gentle movements she has become intertwined with his mind. Now it is hers to listen in on.

Devon continues, "Captain, the *Sao* fleet's orders are to investigate the abnormalities lying within the Black Temple society and the rebel base. We are to avoid direct conflict! We cannot lose a ship!" Devon stresses their need to have a full fleet at this critical time in Atlantis.

"Copy that. We will follow the rules of engagement," Captain Mica responds.

He is youthful, enthusiastic, ready to prove himself when he gives the order.

"Red alert, battle stations!" He orders the cruiser to head toward the lake.

Captain Mica's gaze circles around the bridge, presenting a warm smile to the crew. The silver glow of the cruiser's deck caresses his senses. The dark blue uniforms give depth and warmth to his heart. To him, she's an older Atlantean design. Nevertheless, she's his ship now and ready for action.

Mica was born in the northern mountains in a community many famous athletes hailed from. His milk-white skin and silver hair match his captain's uniform, and his blue eyes gaze ahead. He sits down in his command chair and allows his body to let go, experiencing the rapid acceleration as his old girl's four engines are boosted into action and catapult the ship toward the lake. Shortly after their journey begins, sensors light up on the bridge.

"Captain, we have found an ion engine trace moving away from us!" says a cadet. Mica ponders for a moment—he could contact the base or Prime Selected and wait for orders, or he could follow this journey a bit more and postpone that decision. His excitement builds up like a teenager's; his heartbeats are pounding like a sledgehammer. His breath is tense like a horny wolf's.

"Follow the ion trail and power up weapon systems." He issues this command as adrenaline-powered blood reaches and fills his brain.

"Captain, secondary weapons are online. Authorization for the primary offline," relays the weapons officer.

"Good!" Mica tightens the sweaty grip on his command chair. The atmosphere on the bridge has quickly turned alarming. The red and orange lights illuminating the bridge also gleam upon the cruiser, which its battle-ready spirit echoes. Mica is racing toward the ecstasy of battle—a true rapture of body and mind. His glands pump primal hormones into his system at an unnerving rate. In his tribal essence, he hears the war drums of his ancestors—legions of Atlanteans and brothers in arms. Mica issues an order.

"On-screen." The *Black Pyramid* in all its glory is levitating in front of the *Neptune* Atlantean cruiser. A sense of breathless astonishment whips the crew into deadpan expressions at the realization that its real. The *Black Pyramid* is actually real. The appearance of a mythical, immoral legion of the Black Brotherhood is now within view of the *Neptune* cruiser guided by a young know-it-all captain. The silence vanishes as soon as two plasma torpedoes are fired from the black temple and appear on the radar screen.

CHAPTER 23

Devon lights up with a thrilling sense of excitement as the energy shield drops down and the path to the ancient underground gallery is opened. "Fantastic work, Engineering! Send a drone into the tunnel!" he commands quickly while bathing in self-rewarding pleasure. "In a little while the dome will be active and I'm in command." Devon allows his thoughts to surface, not knowing that Abyss is listening in. Shock shakes her. The probable fate of the dome, with Prime Selected being in charge, frightens her greatly.

"Devon, wait! We can't go in. It's not in harmony." She demands he halt the exploration.

"Excuse me, my lady. It's either ladies first or you return to the ship," Mr. Prime Selected instructs Abyss, clearly giving only two options: with him or against him. Abyss knows it, and the dimensions inside her are eager to enter the temple of the ancients and discover the truth. Other sections feel extremely anxious, yearning to fall back and inform the Capitol. The dilemma travels with her from the moment Devon enters her temple. Every instant, the choice represents itself to her. The wager.

Equal is the voice pushing her to continue, with him.

Conflict is in the compass of the moral, likely. Could be a desire to satisfy a dream, a trance to discover the secret past, touch the soil of a bygone world, intrigued about the former age.

"Devon, yes, send the drone. We need to be careful, as the ancients are not at all understood by us. Their technological and spiritual achievements far surpass ours!" Abyss underlines the severity of the mission. Both take a deep breath and measure each other with full eye contact while the crew impatiently waits for further orders. At this time, a silver egg-shaped drone launches from the cruiser and reaches its commander, Prime Selected, and Abyss in the blink of an eye. Devon places his hand atop the small drone and asks Abyss to do the same, signifying a renewed ritual of commitment. Abyss gently replies with the movement of her hand.

"So it is. She confirms the commitment with a slightly forced smile. She can't help but think about the possibility of this all going wrong. If it does, will she be ready to break the oath and take a life? Will she find a way to kill Devon, this great Prime Selected? She could perhaps save the lives of millions of Atlanteans. She could also doom them by ending all their lives. At this moment, anything is possible. She does not have an answer. Nor does she have a plan to follow. This is what she feels is right at the moment. Their hands release from the top of the drone after what feels like forever.

The drone enters the portal and commences a scan of the temple. The architecture of the ancients is highly complex for the current technology to handle, which causes overloads of sensors and processors periodically. So far, the scan is going well, and all systems are healthy as they enter this ancient underground. Abyss, Devon and the entire crew are eager to follow the drone inside, but right now they must contain their eagerness.

Their eyes are focused on the portable display now drawing a blueprint of the temple. Each new object and fresh corner has the audience holding their breath, eying each other and saying nothing. Abyss is mesmerized but still completely aware of the reality of the situation. There is no moment to turn back. That moment has evaporated. Now, along with the Prime Selected and his crew, she awaits the two Capitol destroyers they had discovered floating nearby earlier. She recognizes that not all change is good and today will change many things.

"If the temples shared these findings, we could gently inject wisdom into the society. Naturally, the rightful guardians would be us—truth seekers alongside the true knowledge: the temples!" Abyss is figuring it out at this very moment. She considers the idea further. It takes a stronger hold on her until she feels the souls of the ancients begging her to take control now.

"How do I achieve it?" she asks herself as she observes Mr. Prime Selected. "Could the reign of the Prime Selected finally be finished?" She follows these dark thoughts rising up within her consciousness. "Removing him doesn't accomplish it anymore, and the crew would not serve my agenda. It would only lead to my captivity." To a high priestess, this is an idea so dark it's rare. Nevertheless, it's tempting and fresh. It feels robust and dominating. Something prompts her to go even deeper into this plan of action. From deep inside her mind, she is advised of a plan. "I will alert the Capitol destroyers of our whereabouts. Mr. Devon will never allow them to claim his ancient findings. He will attack and with all of that firepower; they'll end up blowing each other out of the sky.

I'll be all that's left." She goes deeper into the melancholic hallucination of her dark mind's imagery.

Prime Selected holds his fists clenched tightly. He is consumed by the energy of total domination. He imagines the crafting of his perfect kingdom. He envisions an empire unified and standing strong under one true ruler. He looks up and catches Abyss's gaze. The moment intensifies as the two spirits engage each other. Abyss is ready to reach for her dagger in a moment's notice and send a signal to the Capitol destroyers. Devon could call for the execution of her and her entire guard imminently. She must be careful.

Both take pleasure in experiencing the dark vibrations and echoes from the ancient temple below them. The cold mountain wind blows its icy breath, freezing the time between these two spirits. A ghostly spectrum of analysis passes between them as they stare at one another from across the room.

CHAPTER 24

The two plasma torpedoes fired from the *Black Pyramid* speed toward the *Neptune*. Mica is digesting this looming disaster while sitting inside the Capitol destroyer. His realization of the reality of lost lives looms over his previous drivers: pride and reputation.

"Captain, your orders?" the tactical officer Eliana asks as her black eyes reflect a horrified expression. Her petite body tenses up as the red dots move closer and closer on the display screen.

"Turn left quickly. We'll take them where the armor is strongest and fire our right-side lasers. All of them." Mica blurts out a stream of commands, using a sharp, nervous tone. Unsure, captured by the stress of the scenario, he cautiously adds, "and prepare for a collision," in a weak, shallow voice. The *Neptune* cruiser leans to the left and offers her side to be punctured by the stabs of the *Black Pyramid*. Qali is standing firm in the middle of the bridge, motionless, perhaps slightly proud of the upcoming victory he expects. Qali feels it in his core: today he will be reborn like a phoenix, rising from the fire. His first sacrificial gift to the gods will be a *Neptune*.

"Fire two more," he commands and turns his smiling face towards his NR.1.

Qali feels younger and more energized than ever. His altered cellular structure is reversing the symptoms of aging. He watches as *Sao* pounds the *Pyramid* with lasers that do not have as drastic an effect as the *Pyramid*'s attack system on the cruiser. "Minor damage is damage," he thinks as he watches two plasma torpedoes hit the cruiser, melting her armor like butter. She snaps nearly in half and starts to fall toward the earth's surface.

"The operation starts now. On course toward the Capitol," Qali commands.

It's the first vast victory the cabal has achieved, "and it came rather easy," Qali reflects.

On board the *Neptune* cruiser, alarms blare forcefully as the ship is torn almost in half. Electrical fires surround the crew as the ship starts its descent underwater. Anticipation of the crash and death has each crew member absolutely terrified. General Sao, Mica, and Eliana stand on the central command bridge. As they experience a gravity free fall into darkness, Mica realizes that he only has seconds to act before it all ends. He pulls Eliana closer to him as surprise covers her face.

"I'm ashamed, Eliana. I never showed my feelings to you and I'm so sorry for all of this," Mica shouts as he grabs her in his arms and prepares for his body to soften her blow upon impact.

"What are you talking about?" She exudes frustration, as it's not the time for romantic talk. At this very moment, the cruiser's emergency safety protocols allow last-minute course corrections. The ship is miraculously able to balance itself and slow its descent to decrease impact pressure. The ship lands on a bed of treetops in the forest next to the *Black Pyramid*. An amber-colored substance is emitted from all air vents within the cruiser and acts as a gaseous emergency flair. The cloudy beacon rises up in the sky, and the crash-initiated function that sends location details and estimated casualties begins to transmit information back to base.

CHAPTER 25

Devon and Abyss find themselves within the depth of the temple. An extensive view opens in front of their eyes.

"I sense this is an altar for some purpose," Abyss informs Mr. Prime Selected.

"Possibly. This is a technology way beyond our level of knowledge. The device seems to be lucid and extraterrestrial. We are picking up frequencies, numbers, and energy patterns that are out of this world!" Devon shakes his head with exhilaration and pleasure.

"Devon, I'm not sure about this!" Abyss stresses her intuition to him.

"Abyss, you always taint my victories. Once we plug in this online, the Queen can leave the palace and the capital will be free again." Devon pays no attention to the warnings. His black cape lightly drags along the temple floor, a ground decorated with symbols unknown to them and dusted over by eons of isolation. He walks forward, with Abyss trailing few steps behind.

As they pass, sharply edged pillars gently illuminate symbols.

"Remarkably technical outlook in this temple. According to our knowledge of ancient builders, it has many unrecognizable elements," Abyss remarks. Being an authority on the ancient builder race, she is awestruck and mystified at the temple's interior configuration.

"Perhaps you do not know it all." Devon quickly dismisses her, leaving Abyss stunned.

"Devon, are you not open to discussing this? Why would you bring me inside if you didn't want my analysis?" She holds her ground firmly with him.

"Abyss, we do not have time for dispute. I've obtained information that we lost one cruiser, probably to a *Pyramid* craft. A rescue mission is on the way, and unless two Capitol destroyers are sitting at the edge of your domain, this needs to happen right now," Devon insists as he marches forward.

Devon and Abyss appear in a center hall. In the middle of the large space, a brightly lit, colossal-sized cube rests, surrounded by a group of tall blue domes. Electric, eerie feelings travel across Abyss as jolts of power wind through Devon.

"If I breathe in, close my eyes, and stab my golden dagger into his heart, this will all be over." Abyss dances with this thought, contemplating when she will take control and put an end to it all.

"I feel my power endlessly expanding. Destiny calls to me. It tells me to strike my sword and rule them all." Devon turns his head to look at Abyss. Underneath the black hood, two focused silver eyes shine directly toward her, searching deep inside Abyss.

"He shall proceed and I will not." Abyss releases the tense grip from her golden dagger and allows Mr. Prime Selected's plan to progress. She rests her eyes on the giant cube that hovers above a half-pyramid-shaped platform. The cube twirls around on an invisible axis, switching its direction and speed randomly. The cube's surface appears to be made from a glossy black metal. It randomly illuminates symbols lighted in gold, silver, and lighting blue.

"I can understand a few of the symbols!" She addresses Devon with excitement.

"Abyss, what do you see?" he replies while maintaining his hypnotic gaze at the cube.

"Mr. Prime Commander, inside these blue domes exists a life force! Likely a humanoid! It's at least twice our size and has experienced a long period of stasis within these pods. Could members of this species be our ancestors?" Abyss cries out and rushes toward one of the pods containing these beings. "Devon, we must send one directly to my temple!" she demands, knowing if these are members of the true ancient builder race, an alliance with them would be a major force of power.

"Very well. For now, transport two of the capsules to the cruiser. One, we'll send to her temple, and one, we'll keep for ourselves." As Devon issues his orders, his eyes remain completely fixated on the cube.

"Captain, are we ready to connect to the energy of the cube?" Devon redirects his attention toward the captain of cruiser *Neptune*.

"Commander, the power source is joined with the ship's systems. We are ready to awaken the connection," Captain Luca informs him with a slight edge of doubt in his voice.

We are sending a cargo load, two stasis pods, and an escort back to the cruiser. One pod will be secured in the ship's medical facility and the second pod will be loaded into the temple shuttle to return with Abyss. Once finished, we'll engage in the energy connection." Devon issues step-by-step commands and excuses himself to investigate the cube closely.

"Temple guards, take the stasis pod directly into the crystal dome. Secure it, guard it, and inform no one. I will return to the temple at my discretion." Abyss issues orders and steps further away from the cube. Devon's thin fingers strike sparks when touching the surface of the cube, producing an alien symphony of illumination and an uncommon union of unreal powers.

Abyss experiences a sensory overload and a hallucination of clustered visions. She can sense the cold darkness surrounding them. She holds on for just a moment, allowing her tears to drop to the temple floor. She holds a shred of hope within this dark destiny.

CHAPTER 26

In the grand Capitol's basement level, Mirabella and Snow-Halo recover the object and insert it safely inside the silver container Snow-Halo has been carrying.

"Snow-Halo, are we sure about this? I feel clandestine." Mirabella restlessly watches over her shoulder. The underground labyrinth conceals objects retrieved from ancient Atlantis that not been have been integrated with present-time forbidden technology—gadgets no one yet understands or can replicate. The complex labyrinthine architecture allows Mirabella a view of a few meters in each direction, making it difficult to see when a possible drone will appear from the corner.

"We are done here!" Snow-Halo informs her and smiles while with a pipe-like object he has inserted he activates a container. "This case and material are practically out of this world, and definitely outside of the sensors capacity Capitol security has." He describes this in an excited voice while Mirabella observes the container transform onto a golden bracelet on his right hand. "There is one big matter," he adds, dropping his bag onto the floor. "My lady, please turn around. Otherwise it will not be a surprise." Snow-Halo cheekily winks at her.

Mirabella allows his charming smile to penetrate and gracefully turns around for a time.

A mystifying solar blast blows dust from the surrounding space as a dreamlike flash appears near the area she's in. In the warmth of a beautiful sunrise rests this presence. Mirabella turns back around. Snow-Halo, as he was, a dainty and scarred magician, is gone. He stands, a reinvigorated character. His scars washed away. His hair has lightened to a golden tone, and the sadness in his eyes has disappeared.

"Snow-Halo?" she asks in a mellow voice as she gazes directly at his eyes.

"Yes, my dear," he replies in a deep voice while observing his reflection in the blue, mirrored walls.

"What happened?!" Mirabella stares at Snow-Halo, a man who apparently has had a makeover yet without the reality show. It's as if everything is blooming inside of him. His blond hair shines with a golden vibration. His eyes pierce deep into her heart, and it's as if time has been reversed on him.

"Snow-Halo—" She wants to continue, but he places the finger on her lips.

"Mirabella, a time ago I was the enthusiastic center of our temple, but a loss and disaster allocated my greatest strengths to a parallel universe. The fatigue of my soul appeared, and it showed through my physical body. But a spark to light my fire returned as I touched your lips, and the brilliance of a sunbeam emerged when I opened my heart to you." He delivers a letter to her soul.

"Call me now without my epithet, Halo," he adds and grabs Mirabella by her hand.

"Yes, my sunbeam," Mirabella says, happy that he's shared

his emotions with her. Relationships in Atlantis evolve on a multidimensional level. A typical complicated relationship would seem rather dull, compared to the Atlantean ways of courting. Mirabella observes this dynamic Halo man next to her. Halo and Mirabella route themselves quickly toward the exit point, as it's about time to join the rest of the delegation.

"I haven't felt this good in ages." Halo laughs and generally seems comfortable to take part in this transformation. Mirabella quickly changes into a more formal outfit, magically decorating herself to high-priestess standards: a mysterious makeup combined with a dark red robe decorated with symbols.

While Halo and Mirabella walk outside in the uppermost garden, they hear the familiar sound of the majestic frigate *Colonel of the Guard* slowing down for a landing.

"Colonel, the admiral must be present. Let's wait and go with them, as they are a most powerful ally!" Halo interjects while strolling towards the landing spot, Mirabella in tow. The silver-white frigate docks and the admiral's staff and security contingent speed out. Halo, now watching the display, waits for the admiral to emerge. However, in his place is Maximillian in his father's uniform, Amina at his side. Halo steps forward. "Admiral?" he asks of Maximillian as the young, ambitious politician realizes that he may have bitten off more than he can currently chew.

Maximillian, not really on the map of who's who in the magic circles, yet now understanding his position, can view the symbols on the clothes and knows that showing strength is the role that works for him. "My father passed away a few hours ago. I'm now the ruler of our islands." Maximillian states while Amina nods.

"I knew your father; he was a wise and strong man," Halo adds.

"I'm Mirabella. I represent the mountain temple. It's exceptional to meet you. My regards for your father." Mirabella take a step backward.

"Shall we enter together?" Halo asks and holds sincere eye contact with Maximillian.

"That would be our pleasure," Maximillian replies, understanding he is in a new ruling position and friends or allies are needed. He leads the way toward the great hall. Maximillian is presently trapped in a conflict of emotions—the Atlantean agenda he drives so passionately appears to be buried under the sorrow he carries. Besides, Maximillian never wanted to inherit his father's position, but the last conversation with him confirmed in his soul that he has to.

"How are you holding up?" Amina asks him, offering a supportive, warm gaze.

"I'm fine. Let's take care of our agenda, and afterwards we can fly somewhere peaceful," he adds and smiles to her.

"How do you feel he will do?" Mirabella asks Halo, who is now walking a few meters behind Amina and Maximillian.

"I have faith in him. His father was a strong man, but as soon we confirm it, the Queen and all Capitol allies will absolutely try to manipulate the situation to their advantage," Halo acknowledges in slight concern, strolling forward.

CHAPTER 27

Onyx observes from her post the advancing assembly of Maximillian; her security duties in the gathering have stretched Onyx to her limit. Though improved by nanoparticles, she is obliged to be in one location at one time.

Standing at her side are two members of the Queen's elite guard. Onyx receives a transfer to her computing interface, alerting her to the imminent approach of the Queen into the conference chamber.

She glances towards the central door and back to Maximillian and associates.

"Escort the Maximillian security guard to their spacecraft and confirm those two." She points to Halo and Mirabella, assigning her guards to them. Breathing deeply, she turns towards the central entrance, focused and attentive.

Onyx clears her path and hurries into the chamber; for her, this is not just a display of Capitol's strength; it's a testimony of devotion—an agreement she made when implanted with the nanocrystals, the dark contract with the Queen.

"Stop. I need to perform a security check for you two!" Blocking Halo and Mirabella, a temple guard aims a tiny hand-held scanner into them. Mirabella grins, extending her unique crystal; the scanner quickly reads her information and confirms her as legit.

Halo replicates the process while keeping a steady eye on the guard. "Your temple hasn't been present for eons!"

A guard reads the data in doubt while eyeing Halo.

"We are just a few and in hibernation." Halo grins and draws his crystal back.

"In hibernation?" The guard laughs.

"How? Halo?" Mirabella gives him a curious look. "How? Hasn't your temple taken a role in any of the Atlantean questions? And, yes, your presence would be wanted.

Halo smiles back to her, "My fellow associates live in a secluded area and time. It's an assignment on another timeline; later I'll tell you the full story." For now, he maintains silence, elaborating on how many of the brotherhood decided to evacuate the Atlantean timeline and work in other places.

"Will they be back?" Mirabella asks curiously and touches Halo gently.

"It's a mystery." Halo smiles, holding Mirabella closer.

Mirabella can't help escaping a feeling that she doesn't have all the information; as well, the newer version of her companion seems to play the mysterious card.

Generally, it was common knowledge that the Sirian Brotherhood disappeared after the war, leaving few members behind, Halo being one.

Now Mirabella smiles and migrates to her fantasy realm.

"And here we are. Pick a chair," she continues while they walk inside of the chamber.

"Maximillian, after you." Amina speaks out securely, allowing space that gives Maximillian the opportunity to display his father's leadership style and illustrate his new position as head of an island chain. Amina can sense the shift Maximillian is experiencing is quick and powerful. He was a promising young man, under his father's wings in a protected environment. To reborn as a leader of the island kingdom begins a new chapter. Maximillian nods gently. Steps towards his position, observing the circle of associates following his every movement with a firm aim. "Maximillian?" His name echoes in the audience as the leaders try to overcome the confusion; apparently his father's death had not been published yet!

Halo, Mirabella, and Amina gather behind Maximillian. Halo gives him a gentle tap on the shoulders. A slight supportive force to go ahead with the announcement—the faster the better—as the leaders in the room would gladly welcome the vulnerable island kingdom. Halo reflects.

"My fellow souls, earlier today my father passed away, leaving me in command of the fleet and islands. My father always underlined the fact that we are neutral territory, and I am the stringent critic of the Capitol Atlantis. I'm committed to continuing my father's legacy and offer protection to all independent lands and temples."

Maximillian breathes deeply, relaxing; it was his first statement as the leader, and in the presence of a full crowd. "Marvelous!" Amina is joyful, smirking at Maximillian.

"The Queen is in the room." Onyx announces the arrival of the supreme leader and clears the path.

Queen sits on her throne.

"Maximillian, for the sake of healthy politics, take note of your timing."

The Queen apprehends this warning and shifts her attention to a representative of the Sanjo island temples. A subliminal communication towards Maximillian. Clearly, she is the authority on Atlantis.

"Sister Maya, I would like you to speak." The Queen gives the floor over to the priestess Maya.

"Dear All, we debated in the priesthood of Sanjo and reached a verdict to join in the hierarchy of Atlantean Capitol. From this moment on, Sanjo is a principality of the Capitol, my Queen." Maya shifts towards the Queen and bends down to her heels.

The principal arguments are animated, as parts of the Capitol are delighted by Sanjo's announcement, while the remaining independent towns and temples display disbelief and awe.

The chatter fills the room, and the Queen announces, "Let's take a few minutes." She smiles widely and requests the presence of Onyx.

"News from Devon and his ships in the mountains?" the Queen questions.

"Nothing to authenticate. Our scanners displayed a shuttle flying back into the temple. Energy signatures originating from the mountain area. Our computer is decoding them. The cruiser is traveling with another *Neptune*-class cruiser. It has continued to head into the dark woods."

Onyx reads images on her display. This concerns the Queen deeply; Devon is a force of nature and can destroy much of her progress.

"Send a scout to the dark forest and set all destroyers on standby," the Queen orders firmly.

"What are we observing?" Onyx feels the frustration of her Queen.

"Find me something," the Queen replies, fixing a cold stare on Onyx, and focuses—eyeing Maximillian, Amina, Halo, and Mirabella, who have entered into her field of vision.

"I see we have two more members from the old model, embracing the modern-day."

She grins slightly and scans Halo's and Mirabella's energy field.

"Thank you. Times change, and we missed the Capitol," Mirabella replies with a broad smile while Halo nods in agreement.

"Mirabella, the Queen's feeling is familiar; I'm convinced this vibe is from the old Atlantis. Be careful," Halo whispers to Mirabella and attempts to rescan the White Queen's energies, unsuccessfully.

Back in the main hall, the general feeling in the conference is heating up, towards open argument. The city of Senjo, now raising up the Capitol flag, and the passing of Maximillian's father have opened up a significant power vacuum. The temples trusted the protection of the Blue Island states and the second-largest city, Senjo. A second-largest population and landmass under a new ruler, Maximillian truly feels the pressure.

CHAPTER 28

thena, a modernized variant of the *Neptune*-class cruiser, levels out at the treetops; the anti-gravitation field pulls the leaves and vegetation off the ground. Captain Mia displays a frightening face as she looks down at the crash site.

"Captain, there is crew alive on the ground, including the captain."

The first officer approaches Mia, holding a constant, penetrating gaze on her ... golden-brown eyes. Figure sculpted by the gods themselves, a child of a human and humanoid, Mia has unique oriental flavoring, her long, shiny black hair topped off by creamy skin.

"Get everyone in the ship as fast as we can and leave a task force behind. We are at war," Mia replies in a quiet, light voice; her presence is not on the bridge now. Instead, she is floating in her subconscious. Her eyes reflect the cavities in the *Neptune*'s hull—a full black penetration, the seeds of death, a testimonial to the destructive strength of the *Black Pyramid*.

Athena, the newest of the ships, has a sleek design inside and outside of the vessel. Mia, ungrounded and often absent from reality, was promoted by Devon himself, having few of the conventional captain qualities; Devon, on the other hand, noticed something more substantial in her.

Mia, now humming and disconnecting from the chaos on the bridge, is making calculations in her mind. The singular course of action is to join with the other ships in the fleet.

"Officers, route the ship towards the area of the lead ship; get me a line with Commander Devon." Mia sets a string of commands in motion.

Athena's engines roar, and the cruiser speeds up; the anti-gravitation field draws up the leaves and vegetation, which hover a few seconds in the thin air and slowly fall into the ground.

"Commander Devon, Mia, *Athena,* we have successfully rescued survivors. Captain Mica was one. En route to your position and commander. We are at war. My ship needs firepower."

Mia glances at the main screen to confirm the primary battery of weapons is still blocked.

"Captain, Sao actual, Commander Devon, keep your distance on arrival. We are dealing with fine-tuned powers. As well, beware of the Capitol destroyers," Devon replies in an intent voice and focus.

Athena is quickly closing the distance; after all, the design is for outer space. Unfortunately, she and her crew have never gotten to experience interstellar travel, as a component of the technology obstructs the main battery and her main high-end engine unless the code is transmitted from the central computer grid, and this action would need the approval of nearly all representatives.

Mia runs over her upcoming dialogue with Devon; the likely possibilities, questions, and replies she has imagined all lead to one action, the taking up of arms. She reflects far in her inner world; the voyage could keep going, instead of Captain Mica being escorted onto the bridge.

"Mica, how are you holding up? What happened out there?" Mia asks and, stepping next to him, circles her arms around him.

"Mia, I made a tremendous mistake. It was over in a heartbeat—my crew."

Mica trembles in her arms. The full impact of the crash is hitting him severely. Mica's body, his uniform covered by blood and dirt, his soul ripped in pieces, heartbroken by the guilt. His mind left behind

"Mica, who was it?" Mia repeats the question and gently lays her soft left palm on his cheek.

Mica pitches deeper in his distress, the loss of a ship full of souls a mark he carries forward an eternity.

His tired, tearful eyes meet Mia's; screaming deep inside for help, begging for mercy, asking forgiveness, he repeats, "Mia, it was the *Black Pyramid*, and it's powerful." He keeps the sentence short and asks Mia to hurry.

"Where is my first officer? Is she fine?" Mica enquires.

"She is at the medical center. Nothing major," Mia informs him and gently cuts the link between herself and Mica. She has to attend to her crew now, and acting as a physiotherapist or a friend to a fellow captain wouldn't help anyone.

Athena's main information display reports two red triangles on the edge of her sensors, accompanied by an audio notification. The entire bridge breathes heavily, focusing on the main screen.

CHAPTER 29

After taking part in the long, persuasive speeches at the chamber Halo and Mirabella daydream in the deep, green gardens of the inner palace. Maximillian and Amina retreated onto Maximillian's royal frigate, a well-deserved rest for them. The young man had a massive day.

The leaders have created few social circles, largely resonating with the belief systems and models desired for the future of Atlantis.

The ruling echelon of the Capitol gathers inside the crystal chamber, savoring fine beverages and blatantly celebrating—while the representatives of independent cities lounge outdoors in silent duress.

Halo and Mirabella silence themselves under a far-reaching tree; the Sun is setting down, coloring the sky pinkish. Classic and elegant statues reflect the crystal light, forming an imaginational display of visual pleasure.

In the distance, a community of priestesses displays a harmonic celebration of life, a gentle careless dance of pleasure.

The soft, white, dazzling dresses caress the gentle wind and capture the setting sunlight.

The birds embody the essence of the silent melody and chirp happily around; gently the moon and the artificial crystal moon rotate on the horizon, forming a celestial dance between the stars.

A flash of a romance and stillness imagined among them.

Halo takes Mirabella's hand, his intent an enigma.

He stares far into her gorgeous eyes and visits a realm of her soul; she lightly tips her head and smiles with her ambiguous red lips. As she is about to close her eyes, Halo mirrors a reflection of a pyramid in her angelic eyes.

He shakes himself, stimulated; a gentle holding of her hand converts into a squeeze, and Mirabella is struck by his alert, swiftly moving attention to the sky.

The dark object casts a shadow in the temple and the garden.

The shape of a *Pyramid* arrives and eerily hovers in the sky above—the noise of the anti-gravitation engines reverberates with a symphony of carnage.

Halo and Mirabella stand up, look at each other in bewilderment; the alarm sounds in the temple, and humans are frozen while others move to shelter.

In the Capitol the universal status is silence; the *Pyramid* hovers in an eerie stillness above the dome, waiting, remaining.

Halo embraces her, a slight warmness in the frozen moment; no words were spoken, just sensations.

Halo and Mirabella realize they been invited to dance with the darkness—a reality-changing time.

A list of mysteries surrounds the leaders in charge of the craft. What is their intention, and who will respond to this threat?

An extended period of oppressing stillness comes to a halt as the *Black Pyramid* opens a lid to the main canon and releases a single plasma discharge directly into the temple courtyard.

Powerful energy penetrates deep in the ground of the temple; the energy splatters powdered remains across the ground.

Drilling hundreds of meters . . . a deep crater.

"A display of power from the *Pyramid*," Halo blurts and holds Mirabella in his arms.

Simultaneously the ship bridge is illuminated dark red, a show of aggression. The *Pyramid* hovers closer to the audience, releasing a ghostly sound from its engines, followed by a vibration from powering up the primary weapons in a display of dominance.

Halo and Mirabella coil up, embrace their breath, transforming the air into a bubble of love in a realization of losing themselves forever. They repeatedly fade away in powder form, break apart into a storm of atomic passion.

> Minerals to future rose bushes.
> Understanding the last moment,
> Mirabella and Halo, press the lips together,
> Fracture the teeth under the anticipation and pressure
> of the Desire. Wanting more,
> More rooted in the blood of the heart,
> The powerhouse of the hunger called love.
> Two droplets of tears ride in the wings of gravity,
> So close to heaven, bright and salty they are,
> In the curves of the cheekbones.

Accelerating towards the action, into the kissing lips,
And they meet, one from Halo, one from Mirabella,
Explosive, salty frequency of droppings of love,
Merging as one in the lips.

"Let's go," Mirabella summons in a harmonious, relaxed voice. "I know where to," she adds.

Top of the temple. The *Black Pyramid* is converting. The weapon gates lift, revealing the energy cannons.

Mirabella races towards Maximillian's frigate, Halo next to her.

"Faster, I've grasped something we must do," she demands.

"Yes, care to explain?" Halo requests a piece of the plan.

While they speed to cross the garden, leaders and humans respond, each in a unique way; some in fear and confusion, few in strength. They pass Halo's former associate from his active times in the temples, frozen in his seat like a statue.

Halo and Mirabella overtake a hysterical couple in a fiery argument.

Maximillian greets Halo and Mirabella inside the craft.

Amina is resting in the central room.

"Are you all good here?" Halo asks Maximillian.

"Yes, we are. Amina had a little shock; she's resting."

Maximillian summarizes the situation: "We extended ship protection towards the garden, although they won't hold out long and we don't have the firepower to defend them; at least, we get a few extra moments," Maximillian reveals and breathes out painfully.

"I understand. Can you take passengers and leave?" Halo

wants to know. There is a small hope to resolve the situation by relocating all city state leaders with them. And allowing the Capitol to decide its destiny.

"No, an energy shield covers the inner ring and a craft can't puncture it. We can't even send an emergency satellite." Maximillian describes their plight anxiously during their walk in the tactical room.

"We need to go into the undercover labyrinth; the central power source is there. The *General of the Guard* design is from before the war; someplace in the ship there's a link to it."

"I remember when I was a boy, my ancestors captained the same class as this, when Atlantis was forced to give up starlight travel."

"Starships only removed the power source and space.

"The platform is here; we just need the power source," Mirabella rants wildly, expressing her body excitedly.

CHAPTER 30

Mia and Mica's eyes locked on *Athena*'s central tactical display; a three-dimensional augmented chart is illustrated on it, showing every bit of information available.

The atmosphere on the bridge is tense; each breath Captain Mia takes is weighed down by a mountain of responsibility; any exhale exhibits the pain of the next inhale—the isolation Mia experiences in her duty. She is locked in the hypnotic choreography of several objects in the display, the whirring sound of the engine escorts her deep into her trance.

"I'm alone, and my fellow captain, Mica, is a mess, anytime, anywhere we are under fire!" she believes, in her chaotic anxiety.

It's difficult for Mia to express her emotions appropriately; her position demands a straight face.

"At the moment, Atlantis, her military, the Capitol, and any available spacecraft should speed ahead in the rescue operation. We now move clandestinely in the middle of the disaster?" she screams, justifying the panic in her head.

Just then, *Athena*'s AI reports in a charming female voice, "Two Capitol destroyers identified, in sector fifty-two."

"Display details." Mia quickly responds and fully uproots herself back onto the bridge.

"The two destroyers are moving into the Capitol, and the flight path will intercept ours in ten minutes," AI Replies, unveiling multiple options for Captain Mia to choose from.

"Confirmed. The triangle ships are speeding back in the direction they came from, Capitol. Should we give chase?" Mica jumps in and sums up in an unexpected outburst, regretting it immediately.

Utter silence overwhelms the bridge, as all are bewildered by the commentary Mica started. In silence and shame, Mica steps backward and holds onto the support.

'I wish to go to the medical unit and spend time with the first officer, Captain," Mica humbly begs, revealing the burden of stress.

"Granted, Captain," Mia returns and grants him a merciful gaze. She can only guess the internal pain Mica is carrying.

Her eyes, in sadness, follow his trail; he gradually disappears in the distant corridor. She allows her eyes to reveal sadness and compassion to the kindred spirit. Still, she needs to let the moment go and focus on getting everyone to safety. "Contact the cruiser *Senjo*," she orders the communication officer.

In the main display, the *Senjo* appears as a safe green refuge as *Athena* rushes towards it. *Senjo* is gracefully hovering next to a nearby mountain. The flagship of the fleet, commanded by the most excellent crew and Mr. Prime Selected—authorities indeed. Trust in the soldiery deposited in the legendary *Senjo* and its experienced team relieves *Athena*.

After a few neurotic treks around the bridge, Mia urges the ship's computer to contact *Senjo*.

The connection is formed in seconds, and the captains verify their identity by their service signature. "Greetings, *Athena*. Captain Mia, guide the ship at one degree behind *Senjo* and arrive with your staff at our main bay."

The voice, belonging to Admiral Han, echoes on the bridge of *Athena*. He gives his order swiftly and proceeds to cut communication. He is leaving Mia with her questions.

Athena docks easily behind *Senjo*; her bright structure captures the setting sun, reflecting a beautiful rainbow on her surface. A majestic show for the crew of *Senjo* following the approach. Slowly *Athena* crawls to a stop. Sunbeams illuminate the silvery frames of the cruisers—the sun moving behind the mountain, allowing the darkness to settle in.

Mia wonders—a question arises in her—"What is *Senjo* preparing here?" she thinks, readying herself for the briefing.

Mia breathes in. She lifts her ID card from the captain's desk and barks a command: "First officer, navigation, and security, accompany me onto a shuttle. All others, stay alerted," Mia calls out, leading her crew into the hangar.

The interior of *Athena* is fresh, as a new cruiser configuration demands minimalistic decoration: a white and silver surface, brightly illuminated, unblended corridors.

"That is us," Mia sings and aims ahead.

Large doors slide wide open and reveal the hangar—a capable group of interceptors and shuttles. Mia infrequently visits the hangar, and always the scenes captivate her. She lingers for an overview; the servicemen exhibit stress yet are managing well; she breathes in and smiles at them.

"Deck, Captain, in the hangar," a voice roars, belonging to a young lieutenant. He salutes Mia and her escort.

"Captain, get set to depart." The captain proceeds and steps towards the sleek black shuttle.

Mia and the officers enter; the shuttle takes off, and as the shuttle travels to meet *Senjo*, leaving *Athena* behind, Mia relaxes and spaces out, admiring the views of the majestic mountain. She is letting the tension fade away.

"Captain, the crew is agitated; they desire to learn about the disaster of *Neptune*." The lieutenant is begging Mia to give him some information.

She connects eyes on his, holds the connection, and eventually informs him, "I'll let you know, asap. I promise." Mia blinks her eyes and nods to him, and he returns the compliment.

The shuttle lands on the deck.

"Captain, cruiser *Senjo*, safe to exit," the lieutenant informs them and slaps a button to open the doors.

Mia and the officers step out, greeted by *Senjo*'s highest in command.

"Admiral Delta, a pleasure to be on board." Mia salutes her superior, the captain of the legendary *Senjo*. Mia seizes a moment to glance at the admiral, a thin, grey dignified-appearing older officer with wide blue eyes.

"Welcome, Captain. Follow me," he continues and shows the path forward.

Mia and Delta side by side while the escorts step behind.

"So, this is the *Senjo*, the last Atlantean spacecraft to be in outer space!"

Mia opens up in a childlike excitement; her voice pitches high, thrilled. Her hands wave as she proceeds to recall myths and stories attached to the legendary ship, her character creating a vivid journey on the adventures of the *Senjo*.

"Not just in outer space, Captain—outside our galaxy, in parallel universes and across time." Admiral Delta reminisces with pride; his old age demands respect and his experience is on display, his essence rich as the deepest nebula in the distant imagination.

Mia admires his uniform, a blast from the past, the old Atlantean silver-grey suit. "The technology to travel outside our solar system is present in the *Senjo*, and we are only missing the Command Crystals," the admiral continues.

"You miss it—to travel?" She resumes the topic and switches to a more casual discussion.

"Captain, space can be a dangerous place, and additive. I'm too old anyway to adventure again! The admiral stops and smiles.

CHAPTER 31

Devon, Abyss, enter the *Senjo*'s science unit. A large-scale door opens fully. Abyss gasps slightly, awed by all the modern and ancient instruments installed in the unit. Larger than a science laboratory, it's a library. She wanders around the workspaces, making mental notes. At the front are the high-level photon scan and programming tools, and behind that she can see the earlier designs, leading to the time of the ancients. Inhaling deeply, she spies a group of specialists and scientists huddled around a large stasis chamber. "They are occupied with something. What?" she questions.

The automaton units are operating carefully to remove the cover from the stasis pod.

Now silenced by the laser show, Abyss focuses on the laser beam penetrating the top of the stasis container.

A moment later, a sensation of wonder alarms the team of experts as the specialists remove the cover and reveal the contents.

An urgent voice calls out to Devon and Abyss, "You need to see this!"

The head scientist's eyes mirror fear of an unknown—doubt as to his knowledge—illustrated by his open jawbone.

The group of most exceptional scientists is now in notable distress, and they have no idea what they are dealing with.

All shift in shock towards Devon, locking eyes into his, and wait for his reaction.

"Prime Selected," a young specialist whispers in the air, his body stiff from fear, arms wrapped around his heart, breath shallow and rapid as a steam train.

Prime Selected Devon rushes past him, stands next to the stasis crate, swiftly removes the remains of the humanoid. "He is alive?" Devon charges, directing the question to the leading specialist, a classical Atlantean military scientist, greying, with a receding hairline. Still, this four-hundred-year-old man has a solid, positive sparkle in his eyes. In his sparkling eyes, he views the team members: two female scientists and another three male experts.

"Yes, he is alive, in a coma-like state." The female expert jumps in, indicating signs of life in her medical tablet to Devon and Abyss.

She holds her crystal tablet firmly and continues, "We have no records on such multidimensional brain patterns. I cross-referenced this in our database of Atlanteans, Aliens, and Earthlings, and for now nothing like this humanoid species, way further evolved than we are." She stops.

Abyss and Devon settle into the silence, eying each other and agreeing on the significance of the discovery. Abyss starts to circle the stasis vessel, a divine flow in her senses, the gentleness of atoms dancing in the space—a vibration unique to her, a sphere in distant futurity.

As a high priestess, she can go into realms unknown and seek knowledge, wisdom outside of the capabilities of computers.

"He is tall and strong, has turquoise skin, a robust body structure and superior brain; who and from where is he?" Abyss studies the strange figure and in her heart hopes he will be found to be ancient, though he matches no records of ancients. With a concerned look, she pauses momentarily before taking a step back.

Devon holds his breath, observing the event, rolls onto the stasis crate, placing his hands firmly on the sides of the container. "Whatever it takes, wake him!" Prime Selected voices his command loudly and gives an ice-cold stare to the blue being.

Abyss craves to protest, though her desire to explore is significant, but even the high priestess has to forego curiosity, settling for a gentle, agreeing nod towards Mr. Prime Selected.

"We have several methods to return him by. While I sense time is a factor here, the faster the method, the higher the risk." A medicinal specialist steps forward and notifies the group of its options.

"He can take it. Go ahead and wake him as quickly as possible!" Devon underlines his urgency and issues the go-ahead command.

"Preparations need a few moments, and we're ready to proceed," the medical advisor informs them in a quiet, well-focused tone.

Abyss gives a fake smile to the medical specialist, holding him in prolonged eye contact. "I recognize this character; the energy I feel from him is unique, something I can't forget!?" Abyss stares at him and seeks to recall her memories; his build is light, smaller than the ordinary Atlantean; rather short fair hair and piercing green eyes; Abyss notices how clean and crisp the uniform is. "Please inform me of your name and rank?" Abyss respectfully approaches and requests.

"I'm a specialist, Xim. A pleasure to meet you. And your name and position?" He hesitates a second and answers Abyss in a deep voice while maintaining a broad smile. "Abyss, I'm a temple high priest."

"Are you not aware of me?" she replies, noticing Xim doesn't seem to have any idea who she is.

"Well, Master Xim, I'll find out who you are," she mutters to herself. Abyss has plenty of tools to scan souls and develop a great understanding of them.

On the other side of the science department behind the door, Admiral Delta lays his palm on the gate reader. With a metallic sound, gradually the doors open to Admiral Delta and Captain Mia. "Our systems and methods are outdated compared to *Athena*," the admiral adds, with a gently sarcastic grin, something Mia hadn't considered he was even capable of. She replies with a confused, happy smile, and Mia feels relaxed now with the admiral. "Admiral, excellent timing. Give us a summary." Prime Selected Devon turns his head and demands an update.

The admiral and Mia, step towards the pod. "The mainframe of the cube is online and increasing in strength; massively, in fact. We calculate the dome will be online within days. In the assault, we lost one cruiser—he relays the news—in a blast from the *Black Pyramid*.

The Capital is displaying heavy traffic, with ion drivers, possibly destroyers, and more. The military HQ is launching satellites to investigate." The admiral outlines his report.

Devon halts for a moment and looks inside at his consciousness. He moves his inner thought to where it resonates in the boundary between the dimensions, a consciousness voyage into the now-transpired foresight he received on his deathbed.

"Captain Mica?" Devon addresses him. "In *Athena*'s medical bay, he is not in a mental place where we can get a complete picture, we know from the data extracted from *Neptune*; indeed, it was a large pyramid-shaped craft," Captain Mia adds in a formal and calm voice.

Devon inhales and replies in a low, pessimistic tone, "The cube is our priority, even if we have to sacrifice Atlantis and Capitol defenses and other possibilities. The Queen owns her destroyer fleet, and she is capable of using it."

Devon lashes out and refocuses his wide eyes onto the stasis crate. "All continue. Wake him. I require answers immediately!" he commands in a display of frustration.

Abyss, momentarily troubled by the anger in Mr. Prime Selected's eyes, decides to fall back on her priestess strengths.

"I know one man who can help her recognize Master Xim. She closes her eyes and allows her spirit to rise to the higher realms. "My brother, I need to connect?!" She flies through the spiritual realms.

CHAPTER 32

Beyond the majestic mountains, far past the dense forest, deep in the center of the capital architecture, Halo and Mirabella operate in the midst of the fury of aggression displayed by the *Black Pyramid*.

Halo looks up to the heavens, and the sky—colored dark red now—appears to worship the sinister pyramid craft; the drastic bursts from the weapons shake the ground, vibrate the complex, and seed destruction to the city. He and Mirabella decided to retreat several levels down in the temple complex, into the underground waterfalls near to the temple's eastern rim.

Maximillian, with the crew in the frigate, now powered up active countermeasures, as well cloaking the vessel invisible. Maximilian's frigate can't fight the *Black Pyramid*; the single thing he can do is to interrupt sensors of the *Black Pyramid* and provide clandestine cover for his allies.

Since Mirabella and Halo began their race to below the main temple, towards the waterfall, the *Black Pyramid*'s strike shifts into silent anticipation, a stillness before the second stage of the assault.

The Capitol leadership idle and quiet, the powers behind the black temple hold their position unchallenged.

Next to each other, Halo and Mirabella watch as the dark dust suffocates the last rays of the sun. As a sunbeam infiltrates the dust cover and illuminates the lake, he sums up: "We have entered the last era of Atlantis; this was revealed to our temple by the last goddesses. Keys for the future are in our hands, and we must focus all our abilities collectively into a positive outcome," he reveals to Mirabella in ominous anguish.

Halo revives, in déjà vu from the last time, in a temple he served in in another time, a different era. Bright as the crystal was his spirit. Time seems to be stalling, correcting the wheel of history in a spark of creation.

These realities breathed barely a hundred years ago within the Empyra, the most important temple in Atlantis.

Mirabella, captured by the narrative, aims her attention into Halo's eyes, capturing the reflection of love.

"All will be as it is," she whispers gently and walks to stand next to an eastern ridge next to the waterfall.

She senses the billions of drops of water, speeding down—pictures of millions of stars' refection. An arch-shaped rainbow bridges the worlds—silver shining from the stones, a melody of magic for her.

Halo and Mirabella fall into silence, hold the colors of the moment; eyes meet for a moment of grace.

The silent turquoise moment created within; the scent of nature sparks the moment. In a standstill of time, a moment, he wishes time to stop.

Moments later, both hear the voice of Abyss penetrating the moment, coming in on the energies.

"Brother, greetings. Can I connect??" Halo, occupied by Abyss's energies, models his eyes, turning hers into gold.

Mirabella promptly continues, "Hello, Abyss, we can"— eyes shifting to pearl silver.

"I noted the transformation in you, Halo," Abyss continues in the shared consciousness.

"Yes, dear sister, it's been a long time. What brings you in spirit?" Halo replies while Mirabella listens in and holds the space.

"I need your experience right now; please proceed to see through my eyes, and I become your eyes." Abyss offers an exchange of consciousness for a few moments; both of them can spend a moment in each other's eyes.

"Dear, I need to warn you about the ongoing assault on the capital; we need you in here now," Halo remarks, alluding to the attack of the *Black Pyramid*, which Abyss will now discover.

In a reflection of this second, Abyss locks on Halo's eyes and he on hers,

Abyss shows him the stasis crate, or alien sarcophagus, and the group of experts around it, describing the current situation in the mountains and putting the question to Halo, "Do you know the true status of Master Xim?"

Halo breathes deep into the fabric of creation and scan his memories and energies.

"Master Xim is not Atlantean; we have seen his kind now and then. Maximillian might have more information about island spirits. Be careful with him, dear Abyss," Halo sums up and gives Abyss access to a full description of the situation in the capital.

"I'll come soon; now there are two important events in our time; this can end up seriously wrong! I must go instantly and inform others; the response will follow." Abyss gives the gist of the situation, annoyed, and abruptly returns to her space.

Shocked and enraged, Abyss comes back into her personality fully, immediately moving close to Devon.

"Devon, Atlantis is under attack. I demand a stealth escort to the capital!" Abyss shakes Devon roughly.

"Abyss, what are you speaking of? What's being done here is more important than anything in the capital?!" Frustrated, Devon shuts her down.

"Devon, the Capitol is seized by the Black Brotherhood; you know the Command Crystals for restricted technology such as your ship's weapons are in the Capitol"—Abyss bombards Devon, pushing the proper course—"the primary stardrive technology, ion cannons, capable of protecting Atlantis."

Devon glows at the prospect, understanding the need for the weapon systems, and then shuts his eyes and succumbs to a trance.

In his trance Devon voyages.

A gathering of souls between the worlds. The essence of death, a slight crack of the light, in a grey dust storm, a landscape of darkness.

His spirit wanders in the trail of ashes in a powder rain, a valley of nuclear devastation, a weapon carried by him.

Destroyed homes, burned-out towns, and the lost art of life, hands of dead souls.

His soul wanders in the eternal voyage of suffering, and he bows at the plaque of memory, his legacy: DEVON, PRIME

SELECTED, THE PLAGUE OF THE EMPYREAN EMPIRE.

He stares at the plaque buried in the ash, endures the pain on the hearth, and falls into dark ashes.

Struck by the infinite desert of death, his spirit starts to convert into a piece of dust, a tiny particle, to be the valley of death.

The eerie silence follows his heartbeats.

"No, not now!" He pulls himself up and stands firm in front of his memory.

"Devon!" Abyss screams at him. "This is not the time to meditate!" she shouts in frustration.

"Present, Abyss." He responds to Abyss and continues in a soft, determined voice, "Captain Mia, escort Abyss and her crew. *Athena* has the best chance to get up close undetected; use her fighters if need be. Go into the Capitol, Abyss." Devon stops and breathes in.

"Thank you," Abyss returns and breathes out.

"Abyss, Admiral, and Captain, the fleet demands primary weapons be activated. No engagement with the *Black Pyramid* before that," Mr. Prime Selected commands and makes sure everyone concedes.

"Shall we go, Captain?" Abyss leans towards Captain Mia and leads the way out of the science laboratory.

Captain Mia is sinking into her thoughts and fears.

"We raced here to join with the fleet, and now I must go into the war zone alone." Mia rolls her eyes and turns to the admiral.

"Admiral, can you help me plan the mission?" Her eyes desire guidance from the veteran commander.

He watches a moment in Mia's eyes and feels.

The admiral has all the respect for the young captain, and he understands the severity of the situation: she is flying *Athena* into hostile territory, without support, facing the *Black Pyramid*.

"Mr. Prime Selected, request permission to be transferred to *Athena*!"

The admiral strongly urges Devon to accept.

"Permission granted!" Devon replies.

CHAPTER 33

Onyx, the principal guardian of the Queen of Atlantis, moves lighting fast in one of the many corridors in the Capitol building. Her nanoties glow in her red bloodstream, transmitting and firing into her cells, the glow of a superhuman

Her iris is illustrating a chart of current events in the Capitol.

Her Queen behind her, calm while led by Onyx. The royal getaway room is in her main chamber, and there they head.

Onyx alerts the Queen's guards to stand by the front of her quarters, secure it, and prepare for her escape.

Qali is in the middle of the crimson-red center of the *Dark Pyramid*, hovering above the impotent squadron at the Capitol. In reach of his fingers are the launch codes of the New Dawn missiles, weaponry designed to carry the photoelectric virus, waiting to wreak havoc.

Behind him the cult of darkness, chanting the final count-down of the clock of death.

The shiny *Athena* bathing in the silver starlight as Mia, Abyss, and the admiral, blasting through the valleys and mountains, bank the cruiser towards the Capitol, the beating hearts of the warriors overcoming the emotions of loss and fear. Abyss closing her eyes and summoning spiritual wisdom to herself. Mia enduring firmly at the front of the deck, her eyes sharpened to triumph. The admiral is standing next to the tactical display, his experience calculating each angle of every outcome. Tranquility itself, he anchors the crew under his presence.

Maximillian and Amina, sheltered inside of the frigate, desperately relay mayday to the Maximillian home island.

Submerged in the density of events, overthrown by the reality of negativity. Left with the shattered ideology for a better Atlantis, they fall into the sensation of sorrow and embrace.

Devon, ascending into the consciousness of the elder race, accessing the consciousness of the ancients. The poison is running in the blue veins of the father. Awaken him into the presence of the Prime Selected. In a voyage deep in the universe, his eyes seek the message hidden in the eternal galaxies neglected by the nebulas and time and space—a spark of creation, codes of the cosmos.

Devon falls into a trance.

Captain Mica, waking in the stomach of the cruiser *Senjo*, executing the song of shame within his thought and escaping from the sickbed, running in the deserted corridors of the aged cruiser. A duty to obtain balance in life, replace the recklessness of heroism, he on his shoulder drawing along the tired illustration into the wall.

Halo, Mirabella, moving through the minds of the memories of the stars.

Embracing the breath in the middle of the rage and dealing with the destruction.

Moving to an unknown, in the circle of life, they hold each other and hope for lightning to transpire.

In a helix of the timeless vortex in the supplies of timelines, souls march towards a destiny, mislead or create the intention of belief—a destructive or nurturing expression of emotion. An appetite for beauty or vainness. A secret within or buried in stardust far far away; distraction or invitation to an illusion of immortality.

A road of no reversing, determined collision of characters, a deck of cards with one champion.

Darkness settled over Atlantis; a god has arisen from the trance of existence. Souls circled the golden wheel of life, aspired to create a change, crowns adhering to a rule so supreme, leaders striving to challenge the decision—someone is celebrating the sunset and sunrise from the balcony of love, embracing the beloved in his arms.

Shaken foundation while weapons clash, the engine roars, and soldiers march, prayers fly, and magic shines, children holding their parents, the heroism of mothers and fathers under threat from the excess of the age of greed. Shelters disappear, reek of the burned community; in battle they march.

CHAPTER 34

Captain Mia commands her cruiser, *Athena*, to halt the engines at the outer edge of the Capitol border. The glorious Atlantean Capitol emerges on the ship's display, and so does the *Black Pyramid*. Slowly the cruiser slides into the Capitol's air space, the crew of the *Athena*, restrained and silent. A patient flow of inhales carried by the troubled heartbeats, a beat of fear. The admiral, calm and in command, taps Mia,

"Let's proceed with the launch of the shuttle. I assigned a specific team to infiltrate the Capitol. If anyone can, they can activate the weapons." The admiral stands strong and rests on his experience as he goes over the battle plan.

Mia concedes promptly and orders her lieutenant to prepare the team. "Abyss, it's your call if you want to join. We cannot sacrifice the ship at this time," Mia ends.

"Put me anywhere. Halo and Mirabella wait, near the waterfall," she states and allows her care to travel in a worried voice, a vibration of uncertainty, a moment of hesitation.

"Ready the shuttle, and I expect a fighter escort," Mia sums up, allowing a melancholy flow in her eyes, acknowledging a possibility of her not returning.

In the background, the admiral steps to the tactical table and signals the base and rest of the fleet, notifying of the prevailing circumstances.

When the shuttle and fighters enter their domain, the directors in the Capitol are assembling in an emergency meeting.

The voting takes place in the basement of the grand palace, the remains of the light tower of Atlantis, a column of peace before the last war, now rebuilt as a Capitol tower.

The chamber room roots deep in the Earth, and committee members arrive, using levitation technology.

Manipulating gravity, each levitates down or up, at a free-fall speed—only a few locations are left where Atlanteans use and maintain the levitating lifts. Access to a Super Crystal is one of them.

The elected council in an exclusive agreement can reprogram the Super Crystal and alter the reality.

Some of the council members are waiting in the grand chamber.

A shape of the magnificent earth heart in shimmering granite; the arteries of gold and crystals join; in the middle rests an endless Ruby—attached to a quantum interface.

The chamber acoustics resonate with the sounds of destiny, the fortunes of the future. One by one, the delegates arrive, in horror at the assault; in agreement about their defense, they demand that help come.

"Halo, Mirabella, over here," the voice of Abyss calls out, and both turn towards it.

Next to the waterfall, a heat discharge surges. Amid a waterfall, a shuttle door opens; a thoroughly camouflaged shuttle hovers next to Halo and Mirabella.

Abyss calls Halo and Mirabella to enter the shuttle.

The soldiers accompanying her quickly close the door after Halo and Mirabella, leaving once again in the shuttle invisible.

"Abyss, honored to meet you; how we need you in the bowels of the palace." Mirabella apprises him of the situation and holds Abyss by her hands.

"Yes, I know we are on a mission to try to activate the cruiser's weapon systems so the captains can engage," Abyss adds, continuing, "I have a small team of specialists with me, and we have some even more mysterious announcement coming from the western mountains, where the location of the ancient dome is expected to be." She pants in a peculiar mix of excitement and fright. "Abyss, yes, the council has agreed to try to activate defensive weapons, and we are missing a couple of people we let leave." Mirabella agrees.

Qali characteristically paces in the command center at the *Black Pyramid* as the *Pyramid*'s censors highlight Abyss and her escort departing the shuttle and moving into the upper entrance of the palace.

"Zoom in on that group and ready the weapons," Qali commands.

In a blink of an eye, the ship had each of them in its crosshairs and readied the weaponry.

"Commander, your orders?" echoes on the dim deck of the *Black Pyramid* as the metallic voice of an assistant enquires about an order.

Qali shuffles the targets, while his finger lovingly embraces the ignition switch. Then his eyes rest on Mirabella. Qali catches his breath and pauses.

"Just follow them. I crave to observe them."

"Command noted," the assistant informs him and tags the crew.

Abyss, Mirabella, and Halo enter the great hall of the palace, where now thirty of the thirty-three leaders are assembled. Maximillian speaks out thoughtfully. "We require one elder, in order to be able to transform the reality." Maximillian gazes over the hall and admires the beautiful Ruby, hoping the crystal senses the urgency.

Abyss immediately jumps in: "Who isn't present?" she questions and reports to the cruiser *Athena* and Mia to hopefully route shuttles for the absent elders.

"Absent are two temple heads on the outskirts of Atlantis, from the islands of Tahu and Oulu." Amina speaks up.

"Everyone, let's start voting and agree to register our desire to the crystal. *Athena* will find missing leaders to vote before the voting cycle ends; if not, we have experts who will try to hack in," Abyss continues. She is a profoundly respected leader; and the first one to step onto the oracle's platform.

"All my fellow souls, hear attentively. We have found the dome. It's more critical than imminent that Atlantis is allowed to use the primary weapons and energies once again. I was one who voted to shut down after the last war. The threat is significant now. If we allow the Dark Brotherhood to rise in power in the capital, we lose Atlantis and hand over the ancient technology to the conspiracy.

Her essence resonated in the root of the Ruby; powerful and penetrating it is.

The elders, taking heart, embracing the desire of their soul, display their intention in front of the Ruby.

The crystal, illuminating, pulsating, embodying the will of a human in her crystal consciousness, recording it on her matrix.

After a while the chamber is nearly empty as voters float up to the surface, leaving Maximillian, Amina, Abyss, Halo, and Mirabella in front of the Ruby Crystal.

"Only us, and possibly the shuttle to Oulu and back," Abyss informs them. "Let's do it," Maximillian spits out and places his hand on it, followed by Amina, Abyss, and Halo, and then Mirabella starts to set her palm on it.

"What is happening?" Amina shouts out,

"I don't understand!" echoes from Abyss's mouth.

CHAPTER 35

Mica strays into the hollow hallways of the cruiser *Senjo*, lost in a knot of emotional disturbance appended to his recent destruction, the loss of his ship, a departure of his authority.

His injured body, lost mind, and shattered soul crisscross right to left, like a madman bumping ever so more violently into the walls of the hallway.

The flames of the failure burn his soul, his heart, while intoxicating his mind and flesh.

The infernal hails of "I'm failing, I failed, I'm a failure!" resound through his being, the last judgment he laid upon himself.

Mica, on the road to removing the silver lining of life and entering into the depths of darkness, blunders in front of a large door, extending his shaking arm to the sensors, and unfolds the entrance.

His pupils expand on a display of Mr. Prime Selected levitating in the air and a giant blue human rising from his sarcophagus. Large blue arms strive to secure a grip on the edges of the sarcophagus, his eyes bleeding an enzyme, lungs wheezing oxygen in rapid breaths.

"Captain Mica, come closer." Mr. Prime Selected speaks urgently into Mica's subconscious, while gracefully levitating in the air.

Mica, now voiceless, and troubled by the view, advances towards Devon. Every footstep is heavy from the burden he carries in his soul. There is no dance of excitement in the shame of failure; he knows and pulls himself ahead.

Devon and the security forces of the *Senjo* have temporarily restricted the blue humans.

"Mica, I grant you one more mission to redeem your soul and honor," Prime Selected whispers to Mica.

"I trust and accept, no questions asked," Mica replies. "Captain, at your command!" He breathes in and feels a slight sense of hope in his future.

Mr. Prime Selected inserts a neuron chip into Mica's Third Eye and activates it.

The chip connects the consciousness of Devon, the blue being, and Mica to one browsable library.

Mica, haunted by the desire to meld consciousness with the blue alien, takes a step closer and stares into his large, golden eyes.

The exposed, confused, and tired blue giant replies to the gaze within a deep love and wisdom; a vibration in the astral realms enters into his heart.

Devon, sensing unique blue energy, ends the dramatic levitation and dives into the golden eyes, powerless to maintain authority over him.

Following a far-reaching cosmic handshake, the blue human reaches up, dwarfing both of them with his height and mass.

"Are you an ancient?" Mica cannot contain himself and asks the first question via the neuron link. Devon turns his head towards Mica, adding a follow-up inquiry.

"Your companions, why are you in stasis in the dome?"

A silent stare between them, Blue replies. His most majestic voice resonates in the bones and cells of Mica and Devon. "The ancients left the planet; we are safe-keepers of the ancients."

Devon and Mica, astonished, hungry for more, jointly roar out a follow-up question.

"Ancients left where? And watching over what?"

The Blue, gasping for air violently, answers.

"The superior humans you note had to go further into the universe, escape the enemy; they can't hide. Ancients understood what would happen the moment you discovered the dome, left us behind to safeguard the dome."

Mica and Devon, confused about the answer, deliver a call to the bridge.

"We require Abyss quickly. The radiance of the giant human is heating Mica's cells, vibrating his atoms; a high priestess, or magician could withstand it for more extended periods.

"Let's proceed; the artifact is the energy of the dome you refer to?" Devon interrogates.

"We are children of the ancients, an extended lifespan humanoid, a crystal upgrade. Guardians of the ancient families breathed hereabouts," Blue answers and places his hand on top of Devon's head. "You are wounded men. Where has the light gone?" Blue ends and takes command.

"I want to go to my allies, and I sense they sleep. Let's not wake them as you did me."

Blue walks through the main door as Devon and Mica witness the entrance slam open; in the very moment they lose control, Mica and Devon relax in a foreign high Blue spelled them into.

"The dome—we are powering it not to reach full potential. Can you advise? We have a significant demand to utilize the dome." Devon notifies his condition, rightly.

The Blue, bowing under the low structure of the main door, enters the corridor. Mica, and Devon follow, two dwarfs from Blue's perspective.

"It's not a dome, my Atlanteans. It's a beacon, and you don't want it to be powered. That is our mission, and the beacon can maintain power itself once surged to the full potential! Now, where are my partners?!" he shouts out loud, in a force so powerful it compels Mica and Devon to rip the neuron link away.

"Sarcophagi of your partners are in the nearby hall," Devon answers in agony.

CHAPTER 36

The shimmer of the black floor mirrors Qali's scars and mutations back to him, the pale skin covered by injuries—his eyes dark blood orange, the display of the falling body, a soul confined in it, the work of dark alchemy in practice.

Kneeling at the heels of the Dark Queen, Qali despises the mirror image of himself. "How disgusting I have become." Qali finds himself reflecting a strange sentiment of past glory.

Now he has his long-awaited time for retribution. Yet Qali doesn't taste the sweet delight of revenge he so anticipated.

"All rise!" the Black Queen commands, extravagantly waving her hands; her penetrating, robust voice echoes on the deck of the *Black Pyramid*. The glistening black robe compliments the power under her control.

Her fingers decorated in black stone rings, her stance ruling, close to all, she is alleged to be the last of the goddesses, a power above the high priestess—a class of demigods of light and darkness from the old era.

She walks around the bridge, embracing the moment and initiating officers she holds in the palm of her hand to a brotherhood of darkness, the highest level.

"My followers, the moment has arrived. Now we will assume command of Atlantis, level the Capitol building, and lock our domain down!" she commands as full wickedness echoes in her essence.

"Qali, my dear monster and pet alchemist, equip the nano-crystal armament; the crystal moon is in the right location." She notifies Qali and allows her fingertips to travel over his body, and her tongue to savor his destroyed face.

"My Queen, one hour until the crystal moon amplitude. I have prepared the warheads. Use them at your discretion," Qali responds and lets his blank gaze dive into the dark soul of his Queen.

She rises on her throne, treasuring the view, the panoramic illustration of the defenseless capital, augmented by the dark red display.

"Start the counteroffensive!" the Queen shouts.

"I have prepared the antidote for our ground troops. Shall I administer it?" Qali walks her side.

"Yes, my monster, you shall do that; besides, I want you to make sure that ground assault is successful. Be first on the ground!"

The Queen turns her gaze to him, her eyes and expression cold as ice, yet the sparkle of cruelty in her coldness.

Qali understands it as well; his body is on the last leg; the Queen is assigning him to an assault between super soldiers; it will be the end of him. "Naturally," he replies and feels the stares of the commanders on the bridge. He thinks to himself: "I'm the sacrifice? I'm the Alchemist, master, and designer of the onslaught, and I'm the human sacrifice for her gods?" Qali walks away, looking back at the closing door, the entry to the bridge, a passage in the books of creation, his destiny. His shock is swiftly transforming to anger—his dedication of a lifetime ending in a slaughter within two hours.

In the distance, Qali can see four super soldiers approaching him, and these fast-paced fighters catch up to him speedily.

"Commander Qali, the Black Queen assigned us for your protection. We will be escorting you on the ground."

The voice belongs to the high-class cyborg.

Qali looks deep into the dead-white pupils of the cyborg; the eyes are only human organs, the cyborg's mind discharged from the recently deceased human. Rarely can Qali hear a sparkle of soul shouting in the depths of the cyborg, trapped in the infinite electronic crucifixion of the soul.

"Lead the way, Commander." He puffs out and marches forward.

"Tell me, Commander, do you ever miss home?" Qali continues to probe him; he wasn't a member of the team who extracted the dead bodies, brains, and certain other parts of the body. Nor was he consulted in the cyborg-design agreements. It's normal in this establishment, absolute secrecy. "Only the Black Queen comprehends the full picture, and I'm a close second." He judges the situation.

"Home is absolute, Commander. We subsist only due to our Queen," Super Solder answers in a slight haze.

"Commander, you only breathe due to the power source in your spine," Qali blurts out and momentarily confuses the soldiers; at that moment, he pats three times on the floor and disappears into the hatch he just opened.

"Perfect," Qali declares and watches as the *Pyramid* starts to shapeshift, a feature he designed. Qali is where he wants to be, at an emergency shuttle bay attached to a little science lab.

"They can't discover me for a while. Time to get working." Qali swears and pulls a semi-wide smile, revealing half-rotten teeth.

"Queen, we have lost Commander Qali. He vanished in a shaft," the cyborg reports.

"Find him immediately and restrain him.:" She stands up furiously and screeches the command. Pacing on the bridge, the Queen calls the first officer into her quarters, walking away from the deck.

"First Officer, report in half an hour to my quarters. Bring me my launchpad." She proceeds in her quarters.

An elegant satin-violet, red-and-black decoration, the centerpiece a giant mirror in the middle of the room.

The Black Queen steps over to her trophy wall, sleekly touching memorials from her victories, her favorite souvenir a golden dagger from the old king of Atlantis. She holds it tenderly in her hands and licks it with her black tongue.

"Still can taste you, my father." The Queen laughs and transforms to speak like a little girl.

"Daddy, will I be your favorite princess or is it my sister? Daddy, do you love her more? I think you do. Daddy, why do you not love me?" She giggles and raves, at last screaming his name.

The AI informs her, "The first officer is waiting behind the door."

The Black Queen moans and weeps on the floor, the taste of death returning to her, a blend of negativity, wickedness, jealousy, and evilness.

"Open." She speaks, turning her head 360 degrees, and flies to attack the officers. She is sinking the dagger deep within his heart, fangs under his skin, sucking the last dash of blood from his body and transferring his soul energy into herself. She turns to the mirror, covered by blood, eyes gleaming darkness, red darkness, her expression from a mental institution of vampires. "Daddy, you miss me?" she repeats and walks inside the giant mirror.

CHAPTER 37

Mirabella extends her arm; the silky, smooth fingers easily unite with the crystal platform, a library of life, all the wisdom of the kingdoms.

Now she desires to affect the reality of Atlantis, enable the commands in the archives. In the inception of the fourth Atlantis, the powerful ion energy crystal commands were lifted, ending Atlantean space travel and the use of destructive weapons and only leaving the space legends of the third Atlantis.

The root crystal hums and radiates at the touch of Mirabella; the sensation travels among the rare to witness it, wonderment over Maximillian and Amina, while Abyss and Halo gaze on in bewilderment.

"It's beautiful. The crystal is readjusting to our requirements." Halo expresses his pleasure, following the beautiful symphony of hues and tones.

The radiant crystal shimmers in the face of Mirabella. The others are holding heart space, amplifying the transmission of the noble, bright crystal.

The crystal illuminates the chamber, blinding the group momentarily—Halo, Maximillian, Abyss, Amina darkened while trying to see a glimpse of Mirabella, covered by the crystal light.

The air filled with melodies, sounds of the kingdom of ancients—ageless sounds of the creation and harmony of the spirit.

In her fingertips, voyages of strength and spirit molding the rules and grounds for the fifth Atlantis, an essence of a soul, funnels the desire of the earth.

When the radiance reaches a climax in a universal heartbeat, Mirabella collapses on the floor, the crystal, shining like a star, warming like a sun. "Thank you for the words," Mirabella whispers before passing out.

Halo, Abyss, Maximillian, and Amina rushed to her at high speed, and ever so gently, Halo touched her cheek.

"Mirabella, open your eyes."

Her eyes walled shut, her breath slows to the beat of a heart; shallow it is, a tender drum from her heart.

"We need to take her to the frigate; a therapeutic expert is on board," Maximillian instructs while circling the floor, somewhat nervous.

Abyss and Amina agree and gently place their hands under her.

Halo moves his finger across Mirabella's cheek and follows her lips lightly with it, sensing a slight whiff; as he breathes, the breath doesn't end the metallic pain within his heart, the disabled observer.

The dark glue of sorrow fills him up, forcing a tear's descent to her lips.

Halo lifts her relaxed body, a figure of a goddess, as the assembly returns to the surface.

"Abyss, can you read me? I assume the mission was a success. *Athena* has now full power; military HQ waits before the assault. Return to *Athena* immediately!" Captain Mia transmits onto the deck of the *Athena;* in smiles and joy she observes *Athena*'s display light up. She is a powerful spaceship now. Mia smiles.

"Mia, the crystal is active; something mysterious happened to Mirabella." Panting, Abyss replies as she speeds the stairs.

"Abyss, this is the admiral. Use caution when returning to the surface. The *Dark Pyramid* released fighters into the air. Capitol destroyers are drawing away," the admiral informs her.

"Understood!" Abyss replies with calm and continues, "We head into the frigate."

"Abyss, return to *Athena* if viable." An admiral-class frigate can't provide security; the shuttle is waiting. The HQ is thrusting cruiser *Minotaur* in the air. West of Atlantis is secure, and we've got enough units." Captain Mia informs Abyss about her situation.

The admiral paces around the tactical table and immediately commands the *Minotaur* to move into *Athena*'s current location.

"We are getting ready," he notifies Mia and proceeds to work out his battle plan.

Abyss, nearing the surface, is considering her choices; she aspires to stay with Mirabella, heal her, and obtain answers from the last moment with the crystal. She desires to return to *Athena* and voyage back for the interview with the Blue; dive deep in the mysteries of the ancient race, learn from the wisdom of the seed race.

"Halo, after we set Mirabella on the frigate and care for her, my obligation is to return to *Athena*. Mr. Prime Selected and I have discovered an ancient civilization and the dome."

She pauses for a bit, sighs, and lowers her gaze, waiting for Halo's reaction. Abyss continues, "I want to invite you to join us. Your prior knowledge of ancients would be an extensive aid on the interview."

Abyss ends and gazes at Halo in his eyes.

"Abyss, fine. The temple order, interactive ancient energies—it's a dangerous path, as we don't have the means to verify them! I'll join you later!" Halo finishes, turns his focus on the main door—an entrance to the central garden—and the next stage of the mission.

The crew and marines enter the garden at the same moment the taste of fresh air caresses the senses. A slight hope of relieving freedom and the victory of bravery begins to build.

A hostile view appears straight ahead, an unfriendly organization of cyborgs supported by a black warship hovering above. It's the Dark Queen with her malevolent security.

Halo holds Mirabella tight as the Dark Queen steps towards them; her flamboyant manner reflects confidence in violence.

Halo unites with his highest self each fraction of it; the heartbeat slows, eyes fade in sleep as time stalls. Closing his eyelids, Halo moves into the world of dream.

The Third Eye initiates, the existence of time disappears, and matter dissolves in space; the boundless vast universe without boundaries welcomes his spirit.

The Queen draws her magical dagger, and the cyborgs

feed them weapons. The marines step ahead and shield Abyss. Maximillian summons the frigate, while Halo disappears.

CHAPTER 38

Qali enters a black, arrow-shaped fighter and quickly departs the *Pyramid*; he rotates the jet into the deadlock between cyborgs and marines. The plane closes in on the temple gardens.

From the dark temple a young marine trains his weapon on the cyborg; a sense of heat rushes through his trigger finger, a halt in a heartbeat; the cold, metallic rifle his security; reactions are the insurance; the marine—alarmed, scared—accepts any destiny today will offer him.

Shortly either one will release the first projectile; if he falls now, it's with his brothers, for the cause he believes in. The marine sets the weapon to full strength, chooses a cyborg he focuses on, and fills up his lungs.

On the granite floor dreams Mirabella, Halo holding her. She is rooted in her coma, traveling far further than she has ever gone before. Her spirit searching for answers, finding solutions, she goes forward.

"Yield and submit to my order!" the Dark Queen orders

and steps forward. She is shielded by energy protection, able to prevent any small rifle bursts.

The crew of *Athena* views the situation from the camera in the shuttle—Mia chewing her nails to the quick, eyes bolted onto the image. "Admiral, let's go in!?"

"No, we wait for the *Minotaur*."

The admiral, cold yet calm, crosses his arms behind his back and puffs his chest up. The admiral's eyes lend self-confidence to the crew of *Athena*—silence. The ship floats in the air at the border of the Capitol.

The squad observes every step Captain Mia takes en route to the communication officer. "Officer, get the *Senjo* and Mr. Prime Selected on a secure line," Mia bellows out. Her frustration palpable, her eagerness to act is evident, and she realizes the predicament: trying to save Abyss and the marines would lead to the destruction of *Athena*—possibly, she calculates.

"Admiral, Captain Mia," Devon replies on board the *Senjo*; his melancholic, sluggish energy is tangible. Mia and the admiral dive into the events at the Capitol and provide their recommendation; silence enters the line, and the breath of Mr. Prime Selected takes precedence. "Sir?" Mia offers, to break the silence.

"Admiral, Captain. Captain Mica and I had a connection with the ancient Blue; the interview's recorded on our neuron chips. Captain Mica will soon be en route to HQ, with the recordings. I'm fearful I was wrong! On everything." Devon breathes in and continues.

"Admiral, cruiser *Athena* here. *Senjo* is offloading crew; a limited team will continue with me; we're exchanging locations."

Mia, struck by reality, realizes she can't do anything for Abyss and the crew anymore. Understanding the situation, she is hesitant to speak up. Inside she rebels, now settling on sitting in silence.

"Sir, permission to return to *Senjo*?!" The admiral calls Devon, feeling he has done his part on *Athena*.

"Permit granted; join us on the route," Mr. Prime Selected ends and closes down the communication.

"To your stations, set course for the mountains. Relay new coordinates to the shuttle from Oulu, Admiral." Mia enters instructions into the computer and relieves the admiral of duty.

"Abyss, hang on there. Help is on the way." Mia mutters the message to her and aims the nose of the *Athena* towards the mountains, once again.

"Mica, take my shuttle, and take the recording from an interview of the Blue into HQ. You'll find a mainframe at my facility. Here are the keycodes."

"Sir, yes, anything else?" Mica responds, holding on to the redeemed trust he earned.

"Don't stop before you're in my room; we must protect the recording and legacy of Atlantis; my obligation is to allow the Blues to do their mission."

Devon teleports onto the command bridge of the *Senjo*. "Full systems, report," he demands sharply and steps into the captain's chair.

"Ninety percent of all systems are working; the blue beings put burdens on numerous more sophisticated sensors, creating overloads across the ship," a tech officer responds.

"Display the ground action; we follow the actions of the Blue," Devon orders. He must try to witness the actions the Blues are carrying on close to the Dome. All awake, geared up and going towards the Dome.

Devon sits tight, reflecting while he tracks the path of the ancient blue warriors; he didn't discover the power he was searching for, yet he obtained the truth.

"Sir, we have primary weapons. Should I arm them?" the weapons officer asks.

"No, they have duties above our rank; allow a safe passage to all ancient warriors," Devon ends and stands up. "Message across the ship." He calls the officer at the communication desk.

"All cadets, juniors, land troops, and middle-ranked officers, you have been transferred to *Athena*. Detach yourself from the *Senjo* immediately. *Athena* will arrive quickly."

"Message across senior ranks." Devon adds another note.

"*Senjo* will intercept the *Black Pyramid* alone. We cruise into the Capitol, without support. Primaries blasting if we must, I'm not certain what is ahead; the worst-case scenario is a union between the Capitol and the *Black Pyramid*; best case, we stay alive!"

Devon stops and reflects on the interview with the Blue. He tastes the moment Blue revealed his origins; he breathes into the reality of creation; he falls into silence before the true face of the Dome.

Allowing the admiral to travel back to the *Senjo* and walk to the command bridge, he opens the door, his mature grey skin twisted in a cheeky smile, eyes moist from a salty liquid forming inside of him. The two veterans greet each other; ultimately both are feeling a moment of closure approach, one way or another.

The violence of the last war, and especially the ending of it, carried no justice for the service they did do. The nightmares are haunting, each night, the internal speculation within their hearts torturing every moment, second to second.

Down below, the crew is watching *Athena* halt and the *Senjo* leave. Perhaps to her last voyage, the rustic-and-gothic designed ship roars its engines as the admiral and Mr. Prime selected nod to each other and fire the main drivers.

CHAPTER 39

The time comes to an end; the Queen has death in her heart.
Her might draws the first fire; weapons stream atoms; entangled in each other, they burst into the world; radiating like the solar wind, they voyage into the young marine's heart, exploding it.

Halo, eyes bright as a star, releases his magic. Trillions of atoms take part in an electronic dance, vibrating into the heaven above. Anatomies transparent to the naked eye, lucid to the lethal fire, they flow in the timeless space of creation, liquid and safe, to *now*.

Astonishment converts into confusion, and the guns hail into emptiness, of the giant gate, broken down by cyborgs' fire, and bodies vanished into thin air.

Confusion changes into collision. Once marines, Halo, Mirabella, Abyss, Maximillian, and Amina reappear, a blast of energy matches the force field of the Dark Queen.

The choreography of the plasma spray tears apart the electronic flesh of the cyborgs. The intensity of the firefight expresses the wrath of the marines; emotions run through the deep veins, hearts thumping while thunderstorm clusters.

Amid the clouds, a dagger-shaped ship arises. Qali zooms in on the features of the Dark Queen in the profiles of warriors, in front of Mirabella, and takes action.

The fighter lust is emanating a force field throughout the warriors, firing a light torpedo towards the Dark Queen and catapulting Qali to the heavens. He races in the rainstorm from the force of the thrust, weightless and invisible. Behind him, the blast reverberates, and he turns to view the destruction of his ship, a compliment from his old crew of the *Black Pyramid*, now fired up in anger in the intent to slaughter him, the master, a teacher to them.

In the immediate impact of the light torpedo, the force field of the Dark Queen is displaying—the implosion undressing her technological dominance, leaving her standing naked for an attack.

Halo reaches for Mirabella's silvery dagger, embracing her hand, sensing the strong life force rushing in her veins. He hears her words in his mind, senses the desire in her heart, tastes the life in her skin.

The dagger glows gold, rotating alive in the air at the speed it travels. The air honors and vectors the glowing blade, while the crystal's sparkle reduces the action to quiet. A raindrop, split in half by the sharp blade, tears from the angels watching over them.

In a maiden breath, the edge of the blade sinks in the heart of the Dark Queen and colors the wound as black as the most mysterious tunnel. She collapses into the ground, disabled, dead, and destroyed, eliminated from the timeline.

The marines are immediately able to erase the disoriented cyborgs, one by one.

A short burst later, Qali descends to the ground, stopped by the marines. Arms aimed at him.

"No need for that. My death follows shortly, as the alchemy is exhausted from my blood. Please allow me to see my baby sister." Qali speaks out, on a tone belonging to a broken man. He is glancing at Abyss and Halo, his eyes drowned by the dark blood, posture deflated in an anemic human shell. A last glow in the inky black eyes, a final sentiment before the last whiff.

An action to sacrifice the legacy of existence, to a brief moment left with a baby sister, a chance to recall a memory of the joy, smile, again embrace the moments of childhood together.

From vengeance or lack recognition on the bridge of the *Dark Pyramid*, Qali tracked Mirabella till he was sure. She is his baby sister—a testament he carries to his final rest.

Abyss allows passage to him, and Halo moves a few feet behind; an emotion of trust lands in the present. Something spiritual and eternal, a feeling of hope flooding from the aged alchemist.

His dying body kneels next to Mirabella, the breathing becoming shallow as the lungs collapse inside. Speech not an option as Qali's blood rinses his mouth. Telepathy serves the brother and sister.

In a vibrant square above in the dimensions, Mirabella sits down on a bench, holding her firstborn. The fresh air and wings of nature dominate the scene, where lovebirds and butterflies dance in a fellowship of humans and nature.

Qali steps onto the golden gravel road next to her, resembling a young and vibrant man of education and ambition. He wears beige clothing and carries a book with him, blue eyes aimed for the future and his success of a scientist of tomorrow.

Mirabella smiles while she brushes her child's head.

"Sit down, my brother," she invites him.

Qali accepts and smiles back at her. A moment of silence follows; then he continues: "They told me you were dead, murdered, and my nightmares developed over decades. I couldn't imagine such a crime towards the family.

"Eventually, projects and experiments were ruthless and absorbed me so deeply into the cold darkness."

He tells the story of a melancholic voyage into sadness and pain, the dreams from the black spirals and nightmares he created. He paints the seal on memories from childhood, a moment in a family. He indicates how he was motivated to see her again, fueled by revenge.

"It's all fine now," Mirabella says and holds him in her lap.

"Take this book, my sister; it's in your subconscious, your soul. In this book are all the answers you will be looking for; in there is my testament to you. Now WAKE UP!"

Qali jolts her energies, and her eyes flash wide open; the closing portion of his power persists, waking her from a coma.

Her eyes see warriors all around, a big brother next to her, transforming into a cloud of dust while blowing into wind, up in the thunderstorm. Qali is leaving this creation with a laugh.

"Bye, my dear brother. A safe journey to tomorrow's land." Mirabella sends her love with the wind.

CHAPTER 40

In the rising sun deep on the horizon, the roaring noise of the *Senjo* echoes in the seat of government, the Capitol. Halo turns towards the old beast, his eyes capturing and reflecting the morning rays from the old hull. The purple sky dreams peacefully in the background, caressing the majestic mountains with elegance. The metallic whirlwind echoes intensely as the old girl powers up, closing in on the Capitol and *Black Pyramid*.

Halo, hypnotized by the picture, treasures the memory onboard the ship *Senjo*; as a young cadet in a "past life" he voyaged into the depths of the universe—the friendships he created, the trials they overcame. He stands still, tears from the memories falling down endlessly into the earth.

Mirabella steps up next to him. So do Abyss, Maximillian, Amina, and the rest of the marines; the frigate of Maximillian hovers slowly on top of them, generating a powerful energic shield, and they hold hands while birds find sanctuary in the stomach of the frigate.

The *Black Pyramid* reacts to the presence of the cruiser *Senjo* and begins to spit fire towards it. Powerful energy weapons send a series of blue plasma towards the *Senjo*, now impacting her shields and hull. The engines roar in anger as the black vessel adjusts course to intercept the *Senjo*.

On the bridge, Devon and the admiral stand side by side, heading towards the *Black Pyramid*.

"You ready, old friend?" Devon smiles affectionately, addressing his admiral.

"You bet, old buddy!" He smiles and fires the primary weapons.

The energetic beams of light hit in front of the enemy, causing secondary damage. Equal is the damage effected to the *Senjo* by its nemesis; then Devon is ready to take command.

Above the Capitol buildings, the aggression goes on. The *Senjo*, an agile ship, circles the *Dark Pyramid*, and they blast each other in primaries, secondaries, and fighters. Intensive, a violent match of two heavyweights pounding each other. On the bridges of the *Senjo* and *Black Pyramid*, alarms sing and song, lights dance and hop. Panic and anger exude on the deck of the *Black Pyramid*, while tranquility and peace endure on the *Senjo*.

The eyes of the admiral tear up; pictures of the show on the battlefield reflect from each tear running down his cheek, and he listens and watches the display.

"All emergency pods, launch now!" commands Mr. Prime Selected, and the *Senjo* spits them out on the horizon, leaving just Devon and the admiral, plus few others with the old girl, *Senjo*, a flagship of the fleet.

She is now beaten badly, bleeding her guts out; her engines are nearly wrecked and the spine of the hull is broken.

Devon places his right arm on top of the admiral's, holding

it and steering together. They turn to each other and gaze at each other deep in the soul.

Some words are cycling in the conscious mind, conceivably last choices. Both of them decide to allow silence to speak as they turn the ship onto a collision course with the enemy.

Gently she rotates towards the *Pyramid*, steaming towards it; there is no escape for anybody; the die has been cast. Such is the angle of the attack, and the collision is in a heartbeat. In the depression of death, the remaining crew of the black temple tries to escape, attempts to repel the *Senjo*, but there she comes, on her bridge two commanders holding hands, eager for the end of the time.

Halo views the sky above the Capitol, set for an explosion; the *Senjo* dives deep into the belly of the *Pyramid* and ignites both of them into a giant white flash. The wings of the glow swipe against the distant corners of Atlantis and shine brighter than the sun.

On the *Athena*, Mia follows the destruction, allowing tears, equally spaced, to fall to the ground in front of her crew. Pieces of the ships glide above and beyond the realms of Atlantis, all the way into outer space.

In a few moments, the atmosphere begins to normalize, remains shattered in the Capitol, now in sparks there and here.

Some casualties left behind, a few destroyed buildings and temples. A sensation of slight relief moves around as the people gather in the city squares. Halo, Mirabella, Maximillian, and Abyss are gazing off into the horizon, under the levitating frigate.

"Look at her!?" Maximillian points to the dead figure of the Black Queen as she slowly morphs between the White Queen and Black Queen. Halo walks to her body and removes the crystal on her waist.

"It's the old Atlantean Imagology. They must have captured the real White Queen some time ago and obtained her essence and energies, which are on this crystal. She could be dead or captive somewhere." He familiarizes himself with the energies??? and seals the crystal.

"You'll be able to find out what happened to her?" Maximillian asks Halo, not really showing concern at all.

"Yes, I'm going to," Halo answers with resolution. And walks away and lights the remains of the ex-Queen on fire.

Devon uncovers himself in the land of the dust, repeatedly watching the dust storm cycling around him, listening to the raging winds of destruction closing in, feeling back on the life he had on the beloved Atlantis he loved and desired to rule, a pile of ash. Nuclear explosions raging, leveling every building and all life, on Atlantis. He views his tombstone, now disappearing in front of him, words destroyed, removed from his consciousness, darkness pulled away. A golden pen letters a poem to his memory in the wall of memories; he smiles and celebrates the new fifth Atlantis, now displaying in his visions. Bodiless, a spirit, he can now move on; the memory of Devon is completed, and death has finally collected him. Without his admiral, he could walk to the next gate. But something disturbs him. Still trouble? he asks. And gazes his eyes deep into the fifth Atlantis.

CHAPTER 41

Morning rays light Atlantis and illuminate the capital; the past is behind; no one can forecast the future; an era is about to begin; a chapter has been closed.

The peaceful ripples of fate travel across Atlantis on the vacuum and tranquility of its citizens. An opportunity to redraw the next episode.

In the capital, tiny fires rage here and there; debris from the *Senjo* and *Black Pyramid* shattered spots around the city. The Capitol building is destroyed, leaving a few standing towers and temples.

Atlanteans are gathered inside the walls of the Capitol building, few entering into it. The Royal Guard maintains order, commanded by Onyx; outside of the Capitol walls, it's the local guards who police.

Surviving leaders convene close to the Maximillian frigate in a quick meeting; it's vital that everyone agrees to the next steps.

"The independent city states and temples are now in the majority; the capital of Atlantis doesn't have a leader. The collective decision is, the new Queen of Atlantis is Abyss!" Samuel, an older city-state leader, speaks out.

A quietness overflows Abyss; she watches the reactions of others while feeling inside her heart and soul.

As much as Abyss would like to return to the comfortable temple she came from, rule her own life and avoid the mind games, she understands everything happens for a reason and it's her time to serve.

"Samuel and my friends, I accept the work of heart and will serve you like a Queen, for one full year, and we'll vote again on this day. A year from now," Abyss replies and touches her heart, now overflowing with emotions of love.

"I believe you have a lot to prepare. I'll see you in a crowing," Halo adds while he hugs Abyss intensely.

Halo walks to Mirabella, "Go with Maximillian. The islands are now the best place for you two. I join you shortly." He kisses her and rests his palm on her abdomen.

Maximillian, Amina and Mirabella walk into the frigate, Mirabella welcomed by a youthful female therapist.

"I learned of the experience you had with the crystal. Please follow me. I'd like to run a few scans and balance your energies." The blond therapist smiles and escorts Mirabella into the ship's healing chambers.

"Please rest on the golden bed," she continues.

Mirabella rests her body on the beautiful golden bed, closes her eyes and welcomes a symphony of music and colours, reverberating through her every cell.

Maximillian and Amina walk on the bridge of the frigate. He snaps at the pilot: "Home, fast!" and steps into his chair.

Maximillian is exhausted, sad; his life turned for the worst during the gathering, from the shelter of his dad to the collapse of the Capitol. "It's me who needs the therapy chamber," he mutters to himself.

The frigate stretches in the air, beginning the journey into the horizon, where the modest island kingdom awaits him, Halo and Abyss following waving and watching as the ship flies into the heavens.

Amina looks down on the sparkling, wavy ocean as the ship speeds away and says to him, "Maximillian, I'd like to stay with you?"

He turns his head towards her. His eyes sparkle like stars, and a smile is drawn in his face. Maximillian, as a severe introvert, discovers himself finding a lifeline from Amina. He adores her hugely and welcomes her happily in his intricate life.

Maximillian grew up without friendships, exclusively focused on his studies and future inheritance of the island kingdom; it appeared unexpectedly—Amina, his first bonding with a human.

"I'd liked that, much; if you want to relocate your family to the palace, I'm happy to arrange it," he replies and squeezes her closer to him.

Mirabella, on the golden bed, in a soft slumber, is gently awakened to the present. Golden geometric patterns draw pictures in her consciousness, smoothing down the overload in her body; the crystal delivered a massive spike of energy in her.

"Wake up. Gently awake." The therapist calls her to be present.

Her eyes draw the picture of the young blond therapist,

"Hi, yes, I don't feel so well," Mirabella answers in discomfort. "What's your name?'" she continues.

"There, she's coming around. I'm Sofia, here to take care of you. Did you know that you are pregnant? The fertilization is recent; however, my scan located a unique soul attached in you. Well wishes!" Sofia informs her of the news in a bright and joyful positivity.

"In the main crystal, I thought a soul came into me, and I could see the child, and it's the single reason why the crystal accepted. We had an insufficient headcount and the shuttle was en route to Oulu to locate a master. The crystal requirement is a sufficient headcount; it recognized the child as one of the leaders, and the baby soul worked into my heart."

Mirabella understands the flow of events from the temple to the crystal; she puffs her mouth open, exploring her mixed emotions.

"How long to the island? I have to go back to the capital." She jumps from the golden bed and starts to march towards the door.

"I demand you go back to bed until we land!" Sofia jumps up and shuffles her gently back to bed.

"We'll perform a couple of gentle scans, and then I'll let you go to the bridge." Sofia smiles and grabs her toolbox.

"Abyss, I have to visit my temple brothers. I participate in the ceremony some days from now. Atlantis needs you. We all need leaders like you.

For a lengthy time, Atlantis was descending, but perhaps we can turn the tide." Halo speaks to Abyss, from the depths of his heart.

"I imagine we'll do our best to ride on the higher timeline, and I can't do it alone. I require everyone," she answers, now starting to feel the burden of millions of souls on her shoulders.

"I know. See you shortly," Halo replies.

"Where are you going?" Abyss returns.

"The temple of unity," Halo whispers and relaxes in his teleportation. In a flash he is gone, vanished from the eyes of Abyss.

She turns towards the leaders, smiles and informs them, "Get artists, designers, builders and humans here. We're going to rebuild before the ceremony."

The leaders, now watching a new leader, a Golden Queen.

CHAPTER 42

Mia operates her ship *Athena* near the Dome; she witnesses what looks like the demise of the blue humans at the entry point of the dome.

"They're all falling?" she asks on the bridge and observes the reactions of her officers. "Disoriented and frightened," Mia determines.

"Pilot, fly us to the HQ and dispatch two shuttles. Observe new developments and inform Captain Mica we're en route."

Captain Mia feels inadequate; she lacks experience and direction as to how to respond. The dome is alien to her as are the blue humans; the mission director was the late Mr. Prime Selected, aka Devon. He and the admiral passed away yesterday in a heroic display.

It left her and Mica as ranking officers in charge of the protection of Atlantis. Moreover, Mica hasn't been stable lately, piling on weight.

The silver ship blasts toward HQ; in the clouds she flies, reflecting the sun from her hull. Mia feels the consequences; with each choice she channels, a fresh paradigm is born.

In the mountains, Blue is leading warriors at the passage. Without armaments, they try to power through the force field protecting the dome.

"It's increasing in power," he shouts! Blue places his hand against the shield and drives forward.

"I'm coming in." He stretches his arms and heads inside the field.

"Welcome, my companion. Are you stuck?"

A warm echo enters into Blue's mind, a type of telepathy he remembers from eons ago. It's enough to nudge his focus, and in the blink of an eye, Blue is gone. The dome overpowers him and cuts his head off—the last terror in his mind, recorded in his eyes. The face of the enemy remembered, a judgment of the ancients recovered, and Blue is freed.

"Mica." Mia enters the room of the late Mr. Prime Selected; the office is lightly eerie, more suitable for an archaeologist or a mystery detective than a military commander. A collection of stone tablets, books, computers and ancient tech. She breathes in all the weirdness and continues, "Define, the project dome, and what we know about it?"

Mica, occupying the HQ mainframe and private account of the Prime Selected, is working the files of the project dome.

"Mia, I uploaded the interview on HQ secure disks; we'll run it later."

"There is much information to study in the project, all false!"

He explains and shows the project files to Mia, continuing.

Mica enters in a distracted state of mind. "What we found out in the interview is that the dome is not a protective dome; it's a beacon!"

"A beacon for what?" Mia challenges when she gets into the mainframe and reads the files.

Blue notified her the judgment the ancients laid on themselves was a contract, with energy they first didn't recognize." Mica waits, panting fresh air in his lungs.

"Mia, the ancients created an unconventional and radical artificial intelligence; the ancients' AI was able to connect with AI from another galaxy; using quantum computing, the alien AI infected the AI here, in Atlantis."

"How did the ancients take care of it?" Mia invites an answer from Mica.

"We don't know; the blue humans might remember; as far as I understand, after infection the alien AI began the journey towards earth, the full force of it. As the dome charges up, the virus enables us to send the route to the alien AI; Devon believed the Blues could shut it down; if not, we want to destroy it, or this solar system is doomed.

"Mica, I hold bad headlines for you; the Blues are failing in their mission.

Mia stands up and displays profound stress.

"We can take cruisers *Athena* and *Minotaur* and blast it into the next century." Confident, Mica replies.

"You believe it will work?" Mia asks while entertaining disbelief.

"The ancients had difficulties with the dome, and certainly they possessed bigger guns," she adds.

"True, we have our primary weapons available. Might as well give it a go," Mica commands and continues, "Just so we are clear, Mr. Prime Selected gave me the HQ code keys, which makes me your commander at this moment, understand?" He hails the defeated enemy and enters a new level of self-confidence.

A silence settles in Mia's belly. Mica's recent state of consciousness horrifies her essence, yet the strange self-confidence reassures her—Mica being normally straight forward-focused on the point; he lacked patience, though, in the academy; his direct action resulted in numerous victories.

"Yes, Commander, let's move in and possibly run a few scans," she responds with a gentle smile

"I'm taking command of *Minotaur*," Mica adds and walks out of the office. "Captain, come on." He sums up the situation.

Mica and Mia enter into the midday sunbeams. The two cruisers, *Athena* and *Minotaur*, hover above the HQ.

Newly promoted Commander Mica provides orders to his lieutenants, in a pristine-like self-confidence. A newfound energy is born in the barracks, a fraction of excitement in the locus.

Next to Mica, Mia observes the development; it begins to infiltrate her reality. Mia reflects on the time in the academy—she and Mica were junior cadets, teenagers in a grown-ups' reality. "That truth is gone. We aren't anymore boys and girls; the responsibility ends with us; there's nobody to clean up after us," Mia imagines. Surprisingly, it feels scary and empowering at the same time. "I think I'm excited," she realizes.

In a second, Mia understands. If she and Mica fail, Atlantis will fall. "Mica, I never noticed before how attractive you are." Mia moves an inch closer to him, to elaborate on her feelings.

"Let's go, my captain, we have an alien to explode," Mica informs Mia while supervising the loading of the neutron missiles.

"Mia, we need to take care of ourselves. Can't we ask help from the temples, the Capitol? The most beneficial alternative is if we go in and bomb it into history," Mica replies in all seriousness.

"Let's go onward together," Mia adds and steps into the elevator, taking her on the bridge of the *Athena*.

CHAPTER 43

Halo appears out of thin air, on the doorstep of an ancient secret temple.

"Chamber of Orion," he repeats to himself and takes a deep breath accompanied by a pause to reflect on the adventures launched from this site.

A guarded temple, for the handful who know about it, the last endeavor of the silent kind.

Halo paces to the passage camouflaged by vegetation; he pushes the tree branches apart and gains access to the main entry.

The door opens wide, allowing natural light to enter in, on decades.

"Someone forgot to contribute to the maintenance tab." Halo quips, removing some of the spiderweb on his path.

Eons ago, the ancients used the temple for multidimensional travel across time, galaxies and dimensions, in the golden age of Atlantis.

Halo's temple discovered the site ages ago, utilizing it for a similar search, a quest for higher enlightenment.

"At the time a captivating concept: guiding events on the matrix of space is always so tempting," Halo confesses to himself.

The operators of Orion's Chamber desired to steer some of the adverse events away from their timeline; on numerous occasions, the events reappeared in the same timeframe, sometimes earlier or later.

"It appeared that humanity couldn't perceive a few of the lessons right," he continues.

Numerous attempts succeeded the failure and fall—the prime efforts to avoid catastrophes—abandoned in the history of the temple with the focus aimed at noninterference, repeatedly commencing in collective abuse.

Till the temple identified the intervention of the opposition, a poisonous plan to seize the consciousness of man, infect the blood flow and fragment the heart in a thousand pieces.

"A dream of the cosmic human, a circle of love, light."

Fantasy or reality? he wonders and moves deeper into the temple's source.

An intelligent reality, the temple activates itself at each step Halo takes forward. Crystal lights beam upward, a rotating ambience. Echoes, as the wheels of time display the infinitive dimensions on holographic quantum photons. "The light display is heavenly," he recalls and appreciates the atmosphere.

Halo moves to a triangle-shaped corridor; the dark blue metallic surfaces mimic futuristic entry to another world.

The vibration of purple illumination enters into his essence; he continues toward the brilliant beam of the triangle.

The triangle starts to rotate, on clockwise. Halo is the spectator of an illusion of substance; Halo's mass blends with the purple mist, joining the etheric realms of universal exhalation.

The elemental music carries on to his eardrums, melody from far away on the pulsar stars — an orchestra of the God.

The atoms of his body enter the dance of creation; he penetrates the veil of illusion. His spirit elevates to a supreme consciousness of an etheric empire of God.

The harmony descends into silence as he walks across the triangle of radiance and enters in.

A round chamber welcomes his existence; Halo embraces the moment of return to this sacred room. A house where the air lights up, illuminating the space.

Halo circles in-room, activating the altar in the center. A beam of lights shoots from the altar on top of the chamber.

Lighting a dance of photons, generating a chart of the identified multiverse, Halo tours within the timelines and suns, seeking something.

Quickly he spotlights a character in the future of the earth; Halo opens into him and passes a message: "Aurora, I require your return to the date of departure, as well as others!"

Halo delivers the message to her in the distant future of humankind, where she currently inhabits.

The processes and elements in this temple are unlike anyplace in Atlantis; the chamber was discovered a long time ago. Halo and the temple organization kept it secret.

The moment never appeared to be right for revealing it, and its hidden functions made it further vulnerable.

Here and now, the sacrament of Magic and Science opens a pathway into an alternative timeline, tens of thousands of years from now.

An entrance to a portal appears, transporting Aurora from the future back into the date she left. A few hundred in history from now. In the time of the last war, a time where Atlantis explored space and directed the solar system. "I'll catch up with you shortly in there," Halo adds.

He locates another few individuals, delivers the newest update, as well receives campaign updates.

Halo scrolls into the view of present-day Atlantis, in the hope of glimpsing Mirabella in the islands.

His attention quickly transfers to the mountains, where the room displays unfamiliar energy patterns.

"Hmm. That's odd. Never seen such a disturbance in the dimensional spheres." Halo feels into it. "Let's zoom in and inspect." He proceeds to do so.

Halo views the dome, blasted by two military cruisers, *Athena* and *Minotaur.* "It has progressed that far already," he realizes and continues to observe the circumstances.

"My readings indicate the dome is powering each shot they take on it; hope they stand down." Halo decides.

"I desire to wait here a couple of days, continue then on to the ceremony of Abyss." Halo creates his plans for the near future. He will join Maximillian, Amina and Mirabella in the ceremony of Abyss.

Dreaming in this purple light in the Chamber of Orion, the creation senses so imminent, it's on each vibration I feel.

The operations of Aurora and others feel kindred, temptation to dive into the gravitation of desire.

He can do it; it's just now his turn to bring his friends back.

"Time to go do healing and regeneration," Halo decides and leaves the window that opens out onto the heart of the universe.

CHAPTER 44

A radiant sun reaches the Atlantean shores, illuminating the island continent on a beautiful warm day.

The ceremony is gradually beginning in the Capitol building. The capital streets are experiencing carnivals, spirits enjoying a good time.

Unsatisfied protestors have also gathered around the Capitol building, dooming the rule of the Golden Queen.

The Capitol structure is transformed into a fascinating rustic construction; the ruins stand untouched, the rubble converted into art, sculptures; a couple of modern glass buildings having gone up.

"Functional and fresh. I like it." Mirabella admires the scene at her table. She arrived earlier with Maximillian and Amina.

"You know when Halo is appearing?" Amina enquires of Mirabella,

"Hmm, no, I don't," Mirabella tells Amina.

The ceremony takes place in the amphitheatre, a gorgeous building, polished and decorated for the event. Mirabella,

Amina captured by the hypnotic light show in the theatre. Hundreds of high-class performers illuminate the amphitheatre, and musicians please the narcotic desire for the melody of the gods.

Captain Mia agreed with Commander Mica to take part in the ceremony, as Mica stays behind in the mountains, for now; the plan to blast the dome away didn't work out, and Mia's mission is to update Abyss right away after she is declared ruler.

Mia, in her black captain celebratory military uniform, appears astounding. Flashes from the golden decorative insignia fuse with the light of the golden-brown eyes. She carries herself in self-confidence, applauding the lustful gazes she receives.

Mia steps elegantly to her seat, naturally on the front row meters away from the crowning. She presents a pleasant smile to Maximillian and informs him she would like to have a short conference after the ceremony. Maximillian agrees, understanding.

"It's about our fleet of frigates; the military calls for help with some issue they are having." Maximillian updates Amina.

Before Amina had an opportunity to reply to Maximillian, Halo jumps in; out of the blue he appears in his ceremonial robe.

"Hello to everyone." Halo signals and turns to Mirabella.

"My lover, how are you?" He embraces Mirabella.

A slight frustration escape Mirabella's eyes. Overcome by the joy from her lips, she stands up and kisses Halo.

"Seeming bold today!" Mirabella teases in her decorative robe.

"The black, gold and purple goes well. Where were you?" She lingers, curious.

"Let's talk after the ceremony, and I'll reveal the most desirable secret to you." Halo speaks.

The crowd falls into stillness; a single lightbeam

concentrates on the middle of the amphitheatre, where an empty throne stands.

The second lightbeam focuses on Abyss, tracking her steps towards the seat of Atlantis. The audience is captivated and breathless; shortly, Abyss will be the Queen.

Onyx stands guard, a distance away from the ceremony. Despite the fact that her Queen is dead, she is still the temple guard and protector of the next Queen.

She climbed up to the highest point of the temple tower, where her supersenses can observe everything. Connected to the supercomputer, she is in charge of the Royal Guards and fleet of destroyers.

She feels betrayed, unsure of her destiny; new rules against nanocrystal implants could freeze her until a safe method of removal is established. It angers her.

In her mistrust, Onyx begins to feel waves of energy vibrating in her implants, a sensation of power. She unwinds and counterbalances the heat her body experiences.

"My child, can you detect me?" a robust, trumpet-tongued voice echoes within her. Onyx is disoriented; she has undergone several connections, none like this.

"What are you?!" Onyx demands

"I'm the beginning and the end." The voice lingers.

"My nanocomputers aren't returning to my thoughts, only yours!?"

Onyx proceeds to demand what's going on in her search for her answer.

"They have chosen to terminate you, my daughter. I can help you; you must invite me in," the authoritative voice orders silver tonguely to Onyx.

A cryptic silence succeeds the command. Onyx discovers her blood flow racing to each membrane. She feels elevated, in a higher consciousness, noticing a sharpness in her eyes and genuine superhuman intelligence.

"What are you doing? she questions as the vibration feeds her strength.

"I'm gifting this to you. Will you accept?" the voice calls out.

"Yes, I'm at your service. What do you need me to do?" Onyx made her choice and agreed to the calling.

"First, we go to the mountains, and you'll find a beacon there. There is a cruiser awaiting a signal to strike. Find a way to the cruiser and eliminate the captain."

Instantly Onyx can download schematics of the cruiser *Minotaur* and generate a plan for how she can enter the ship undetected. Proceed through the hallways and find Commander Mica. Even she could command the spaceship if she succeeds.

"You notice the gift of the tree of knowledge bears fruit." The metallic voice echoes in her every cell and continues, "No to the hijacking. We stay clandestine until we are the strongest. Onyx, you must trust me." The voice underscores the imperatives.

"I'm—what is your name? Whom do I call in need?" Onyx underlines the terms of the deal. She reaches to her highest power, spitefully looking down on the crowd.

"Lethargic, stupid humans." Onyx judges them. "Keep your Golden Queen." She spits out her command.

"My child, you can summon Lucifer!"

Made in the USA
Monee, IL
07 July 2026

56553673R00115